WANDERER

Glamour

A Novel: Vol. I.

WANDERER

Glamour
A Novel: Vol. I.

ISBN/EAN: 9783337067007

Printed in Europe, USA, Canada, Australia, Japan

Cover: Foto ©Andreas Hilbeck / pixelio.de

More available books at **www.hansebooks.com**

GLAMOUR.

A Novel.

BY

WANDERER,

AUTHOR OF 'FAIR DIANA,' 'ACROSS COUNTRY,' ETC.

IN THREE VOLUMES.
VOL. I.

ARDVA QVÆ PVLCRA

LONDON:
SWAN SONNENSCHEIN AND CO.
PATERNOSTER SQUARE.
1885.

CONTENTS OF VOL. I.

CHAPTER			PAGE
I. THE CONSULATE	.	.	1
II. EARLY TROUBLES	.	.	19
III. THE STENT CLAN			36
IV. TO LOVE OR NOT TO LOVE!	.	.	62
V. TWO BEFORE AND TWO AFTER			76
VI. A VERY GOOD BALL	.		89
VII. THE CASINO NOBILE	.		117
VIII. 'SANTA LUCIA'	.	.	133
IX. SAN CRISTOFORO	.	.	141
X. WHAT THE STENTS SAID	.		156
XI. WHAT THEY SAID AT PORTINO	.		171
XII. THE MAIDEN'S SECRET	,	.	189
XIII. THE MESHES ARE WOVEN	.		206
XIV. RONALD ASKS QUESTIONS	.	.	223
XV. THE CONSUL'S OPINION	.	.	239
XVI. A CHARADE	.	.	256

GLAMOUR.

CHAPTER I.

THE CONSULATE.

PORTINO was brilliant in the sunlight. The blue sea was sparkling, the houses glaring so white that it was positively painful to look at them. The grey olive trees that dotted the rocky hill sides were too distant to offer the eye any relief. Great clouds of dust rose on the road which skirted the harbour. The dust whirled and twisted into columns; some tall and thin others short and wide. Then, for a minute, there would be a calm, and the wayfarers, hurrying along with the corner of their cloaks thrown across the shoulder, would remove their hand from the broad felt hat most affected in Portino. It was a thorough March day—a day of cold piercing Tramontana.

In a house overlooking the port—a house constructed to withstand heat rather than cold, with a wide piazza towards the sea, and a square garden surrounded by a colonnade behind—was a room which showed that its inhabitants knew something of the comforts of northern climes. The red-tiled floor was covered with a soft carpet, and there was a grate in the fireplace. Instead of the usual little bit of green wood hissing and spluttering and smoking, there was a goodly glow of Newcastle coal. The old-fashioned chairs were not set in a formidable row against the walls, but dotted about the room, so as to take away as much as possible from its bareness. There were several tables—some strewn with books and newspapers; others with ladies' work, photographic albums, and knick-knacks. Though the place would not have appeared very attractive to those accustomed to a good English home, it formed a pleasing contrast to the cold stateliness of most Portino drawing-rooms. The flag which waved over this house was a sufficient explanation of its comparative comfort, for her Britannic Majesty's Consul at Portino was the tenant; and on this windy morning, her Britannic Majesty's Consul's wife was sitting at the fire, mending sundry garments and talking to her son, a tall young man, who was idly looking out of the window at the white sails dotted about the entrance to the harbour, struggling to beat in against the strong wind from the mountains.

'Teresina says it was a very good ball last night,' remarked the lady, scarcely glancing up from her work.

She was a woman of what is termed middle age, wearing her grey hair in two large, stiff curls on each side of her clever and still smooth face. She was clad in a substantial dark woollen gown, cut after the fashion of twenty years ago.

'Yes, I suppose it was,' assented her son, without turning his head.

'*You* enjoyed it, at all events, Ronald,' remarked Mrs. Lascelles rather sharply.

Something in his mother's tone made the youth look round.

'Why should *I* have enjoyed it so particularly?'

Mrs. Lascelles put her work down for a moment. 'Teresina says you danced the whole evening with Miss Edith Woodall, so I suppose you liked it. Young men generally enjoy a ball if they are able to dance as much as they wish with the girl they prefer.'

'She is very nice,' said Ronald quietly.

'Very. I quite agree with you, my dear boy,' answered Mrs. Lascelles. 'And she will be very well off, I should think.'

'I suppose so,' replied her son indifferently.

'She will spend the evening here to-morrow,' continued Mrs. Lascelles. 'Teresina is going to have a few of her friends, and I have told her to ask Edith Woodall and her brother. Of course you will stop at home, Ronald.'

'Why not? There is nothing to do anywhere else.'

'You do not seem to care much,' Mrs. Lascelles went on.

'Oh yes, I do!' replied the young man. 'Teresina's evenings are pleasant enough, and there is no special temptation in Portino to take me away.'

'You find it dull here, Ronald?' asked his mother.'

'Beastly!' was the emphatic reply.

'Well, much as I like having you here, dear boy, I should be glad if you could find something better than Somerset House to take you away.'

'There is not much chance of that,' answered Ronald.

'I do not know. There might be, if you tried.'

'You know that I *have* tried, mother, for ever so

long,' said Ronald wearily, as he quitted the window and stretched himself out in his father's vacant arm-chair.

'I know, I know!' exclaimed Mrs. Lascelles hastily, not wishing to dwell on the time and money her son had spent in England, employed on uncongenial, ill-paid work. 'But possibly, *now*, something might be arranged.'

'Why now, particularly?' asked he, waking up, and at last appearing to take some interest in what his mother was saying.

'Surely you can guess, Ronald?'

Mrs. Lascelles put down her work on her knees, and looked at her son sharply.

'I cannot, dear mother,' he replied, coming over and sitting down on a low stool by her side. 'Tell me all about it. Has my father heard of anything suitable?'

'No,' answered she, gently placing her hand on the

youth's curly head. 'But there are other channels besides your father's influence, which, by-the-by,' she added with a sigh, 'I am afraid we have always rather overrated.'

'Have *you* heard of anything, mother?'

'Well, I have heard, and I have not. That is to say, the matter is quite in your hands.'

'What *do* you mean? Please tell me, and explain the riddle!' exclaimed Ronald.

'My dear boy, surely you like Edith Woodall, do you not?'

'What on earth has Edith Woodall got to do with it?'

'Everything,' said Mrs. Lascelles. 'You are fond of her, and I am sure she cannot help liking you,' stroking his hair fondly. 'Well, Mr. Woodall makes no secret of his intentions. If his daughter marries some one of whom he approves, she will have ten thousand pounds settled on her, and her husband will get a share in the bank.'

'Oh !' exclaimed Ronald.

'Yes; and what is more, as Mr. Woodall is very anx-
ious to return to England, the lucky young man whom
Edith accepts will soon have charge of the whole
Italian business.   It's a splendid opening, Ronald.'

'It would mean living at Portino all one's life,' said
the young man, not very joyfully.

'Well, not *all* one's life, exactly,' answered his
mother.   'And think of the joy it would be for your
father and me to have you settled happily and comfortably near us !'

'You are in a great hurry, mother !' laughed Ronald.
'In the first place, perhaps Miss Woodall would not
have me.'

'There is not much doubt about *that*,' replied Mrs.
Lascelles, looking proudly at her son.   Indeed, though
of course she was prejudiced in his favour, there were
few young men in Portino, whether English or Italian,
whose appearance was as prepossessing as his.   Tall,

well-grown, with clear complexion, bronzed by out-door pursuits, a soft chestnut beard, and gentle brown eyes, whose lazy, kind glances could not possibly be consistent with anything but pleasant manners and a good heart, Ronald was a son of whom any mother had a right to be proud.

'Well,' continued he, 'secondly, Mr. Woodall might refuse his consent. In fact, I'm sure he would not allow it. I have nothing in the world——'

'Your father gives you an allowance,' interrupted Mrs. Lascelles. 'He would certainly continue it gladly, if you were to make so excellent a match.'

'My poor father has always done his best for me; more, far more than I deserved,' answered Ronald rather sadly. 'But that allowance might, you know, cease any day. He might no longer be able to afford it. Teresina will soon want a *trousseau* and a *dot*, and she may not be as lucky as Clara; or——' Ronald was going to add that his father was getting old, and might be obliged to resign before he was entitled to a full pension. But he stopped in time.

'Do not worry yourself about all that, Ronald. Your father will endeavour to arrange these matters with Mr. Woodall. You know they are very old friends, and in early days, before this great revolution, and before we thought of United Italy, and when there were often disturbances and so on, the bank was not so prosperous as it is now, and your father had many opportunities of serving Mr. Woodall.'

'Very well; we will suppose that the father consents, and behaves like a fairy godmother,' said Ronald. 'There is one other objection.'

'What, my dear boy?' asked Mrs. Lascelles anxiously.

'I do not know whether *I* shall consent,' replied he.

'Nonsense, Ronald! Why, you like her! You ought to be delighted to have the chance.'

'Oh yes; I like her—of course I like her. But there's a difference between liking a girl and wanting to marry her.'

'You mean that you are not in love with her? I would never wish you to marry a girl you could not love. But she is so nice, so thoroughly good, so clever and so attractive, that I feel sure you will be over head and ears in love with her long before the wedding-day.'

The young man laughed.

'She is not pretty,' he remarked.

'Not exactly what is termed pretty, I agree with you,' said his mother. 'But she has beautiful eyes and a charming figure.'

'Yes,' assented Ronald. 'But she's got an awful big mouth and a very long nose.'

Mrs. Lascelles looked almost severe.

'My dear boy,' she observed sententiously, 'you can't get perfection. You are seven-and-twenty, and you have been about the world a good deal for your age.   Have you ever seen an absolutely beautiful girl with ten thousand pounds and a share in a good bank, and lots more money to come by-and-by ?'

‘ Yes,’ answered Ronald ; ‘ and more, too.’

‘ Oh !   Then you have been luckier than most people.   I do not remember many beautiful heiresses. But, among those you have seen, is there one that would have married you ?'

‘ Perhaps,’ replied the young man, rather fatuously, ‘ if I had asked.’

‘ And would you have got the fortune as well ?'

‘ Probably not, mother,’ answered Ronald.   ‘ I was, and am decidedly, a detrimental.   There was Miss Caulfield, whom I met two years ago at Scarborough. She was very good-looking and awfully jolly.   We got on capitally together, and I had just made up my mind to propose at the first opportunity.   But then old Caulfield came from Bradford, or some dirty place like it, where he makes worsted, and he found out all about me, and they went away at once—I don't know where to.'

'Any more?' asked Mrs. Lascelles, rather amused at the recital of her son's *bonnes fortunes*—or the reverse.

'Well, there was that glorious American girl last season. I was on Grandchester's drag at Ascot, and he introduced me to her. She was very fetching—really beautiful, and as clever as anyone I ever met. She had read everything, and went everywhere, and dressed wonderfully well. And she did not talk through her nose a bit. They say she had half a silver mine and a whole oil-pit somewhere.'

'What happened, dear?' inquired the mother.

'Nothing happened. That was just it. I was dreadfully spooney on her, and took her about to museums and shows, and all sorts of places, which those American girls think quite proper. I suppose her mother thought that, as I was in Grandchester's set, I must be a relation to an earl, or something of that sort. One day I told the girl all about myself, and all of us, and the next day at Lords' the mother cut me dead.'

'What has become of her?' asked Mrs. Lascelles.

'She has been travelling about, I believe. Anyhow, she is intended for a viscount at least. Mrs. Monson wants to get into Society with a big S. So I was not in it.'

'In what?' asked Mrs. Lascelles innocently.

'Oh, in the race for Miss Alma Monson!'

'Then, after all, it is not so easy to find a nice girl— mind, I mean a *thoroughly* good, clever, and amiable girl—with money : is it, Ronald?'

'N—no,' replied the young man.

'Then you will try your luck with Edith?' Mrs. Lascelles went on.

' Not yet, mother.   I must think it over.'

' By all means, my boy,' answered she.   ' God forbid that I should wish you to do anything hasty, or that you should marry some one whom you could not love dearly !'

She stooped down and kissed her son on his fore-head and lips.   Ronald rose, and saying, ' Good-bye, mother—I shall go out and see if I can get an hour's walk without being blown off my feet,' left the room.

He turned out of the bright dusty Via Marina, where the high wind made the walking inconvenient and reflection impossible, to ascend one of the narrow and comparatively sheltered little streets of the old town. Habit made it easy and almost mechanical for him to avoid the strings of loaded mules, to pass unheeded the noisy old women at their tiny stalls, to wave aside im-portunate beggars, and to thread without any collisions the small crowds of men who, every here and there, were quarrelling violently, and appeared to be on the verge of a murderous fight. Three months ago he could not have ascended the steep hill so quickly. He had not then learnt to view the street disputes with indifference. When fresh from London, he used to fear that at any moment knives would be drawn and fearful wounds inflicted. He had now become accustomed to the melancholy tale of misery which every successive beggar unfolded—and in Portino more than half the population seemed to be beggars. Their lamentations produced no greater impression on his mind than the babbling of a brook. Perhaps this morning his gestures of refusal were more impatient than usual, for even the babbling of a brook may irritate, if the nerves are in a high state of tension and the mind is pre-occupied. As he ascended, the street became less crowded. There were many corners absolutely deserted, for round them the Tramontana whistled and howled and picked up the dust, and the fragments of decayed vegetables, and bits of paper, and flung them about wildly. Soon Ronald reached the place he had fixed on to spend a quiet hour. It was a sunny terrace much frequented by the *Portinesi* on mild afternoons, but now, on this stormy morning, quite deserted. The great block of the Palazzo Alfieri, with its wide-stretching colonnades and its numerous offices, sheltered the long narrow garden on the north side and cut off the cruel wind. A small grove of orange trees, where the band played in the summer evenings, closed the one opening through which the Tramontana might have crept in and swept the garden. It was high up above the narrow streets, and from its parapet you looked over the terraced roofs of the town, and the courtyards of the Palazzi, right down to the blue waters of the harbour. One glance along the gravel walk told Ronald that there was no one here to disturb his thoughts.

They were not as entirely pleasant as might be supposed. When a young man hears that he has the chance of winning an attractive girl, whose hand will not only bestow on him domestic happiness, but also a comfortable fortune and a good position, he ought to look more cheerful than did Ronald on this March morning. He was not, just now, disposed to be particularly cheerful, for his mind dwelt on the past rather than the future, and the retrospect was not entirely satisfactory.

CHAPTER II.

EARLY TROUBLES.

MR. LASCELLES had been British Consul at Portino for many years, after having served in the Colonial office and as Vice-Consul at various Italian towns. His private means were small, and living on his official income, he spent what he could spare in educating his children in England. Ronald was first sent to an excellent private school, and then to Exminster, which is neither as expensive nor as fashionable as Eton or Harrow, but at the time of our story, was known for its high tone, the thoroughness of the instruction conveyed, and the admirable discipline enforced by its head master. Winning an entrance scholarship,

2—2

Ronald proceeded to Cambridge, where the early successes he obtained gladdened the heart of his parents, and encouraged the most sanguine hopes for his future career. But though Ronald worked hard at times, he was not, at that period, capable of any long sustained effort. He could stick to his books, attend lectures, and read with his private tutor, for a whole term, never indulging in any relaxation except what was necessary for his health. But then he would consign all books and all work to entire oblivion, and extend his holiday far beyond the vacation, until the day approached when 'term divides,' and even until he could count the hours to the next examination. Then there would be a violent reaction, and once more he would rise with the sun, make notes, solve problems, commit to memory unceasingly, endeavour to compress into four weeks the work of as many months. The result may be guessed. He passed in mathematical honours, but he failed to gain a higher place than that of twenty-sixth wrangler. Several men in his own college, whose abilities were inferior to his own, obtained, by their perseverance, prior claims to the fellowship he had hoped for. Ronald had desired to go to the Bar, but his father's means would, as he well knew, not suffice to keep him till briefs came. The fellowship was to help over the interval—and the fellowship escaped him. To what should he now turn? It was imperative to do something and to earn his living. The Indian Civil Service was suggested. But Mrs. Lascelles objected to her only son going into exile for the best years of his life, and Ronald was quite willing to obey his mother's wishes. He had no special wish to leave Europe for an indefinite time, and no ambition to dispense justice to natives in some remote district, where he would be forgotten by all except his nearest relatives. Mr. Lascelles exerted his influence to obtain for his son some Government appointment. An *attachéship*, leading possibly to the higher posts of diplomatic service, was closed to Ronald, because, even more than the beginnings of a liberal profession, such a post required an ample private income. Wherefore, after an interval of idleness which Ronald spent, like many other young men, in London, without doing any special mischief, but also without doing himself or anyone else any good, he presented himself as a candidate for Somerset House. The examination was, as he termed it somewhat conceitedly, a mere 'exercise canter.' If his school and university training had done nothing else, it had, at any rate, accustomed him to the 'mill' of cramming up for almost any public trial which might be required of him. So the nomination was speedily confirmed, and the invalid nobleman to whose influence it was due, wrote a courteous letter to Mr. Lascelles, congratulating him on his son's brilliant success. The British Consul was often able to serve even influential persons who came to Portino for their health. When Italy was still split up into a number of small states, the simmering elements of revolution, which burst out into occasional revolts so many times before they culminated in the great war of 1859, kept the various little monarchies in a constant condition of fidgety unrest. Police regulations were tyrannical and inquisitorial; strangers, even wealthy strangers, were often driven to the verge of despair by petty vexations and tedious delays. Mr. Lascelles did what he could to grease the wheels. Though a man of no very distinguished ability, his unfailing good temper and tact enabled him to keep on good terms with the various officials, whatever might be the changes in the *personnel* of the administration. And he was always ready to soothe an angry traveller, to help him over his difficulties, to make his stay agreeable, and to facilitate his departure. Mr. Lascelles, therefore, had many friends, and it was one of these who obtained a nomination for Ronald.

One hundred pounds a year is not very much, even when translated into Italian currency. But when it represents the total income of a young gentleman whose ideas of life were formed at Exminster and Cambridge, it is very little indeed. Ronald was not a spendthrift, but he had not learnt to economize. Introduced to many pleasant families by his father's letters, he soon became one of the regular men about town in a set only a little less expensive than the most fashionable. He was good-looking and pleasant; he danced well and was willing to make himself useful. Hence, though his circumstances were pretty well known, he was asked out everywhere.

Mr. Lascelles was quite aware that his son could not make his salary suffice for his wants, and therefore supplemented it by as much as he could afford—another hundred and fifty. On this Ronald had to manage as best he could. He knew his father's position, and was well aware that getting into debt meant a curtailment of comforts for his parents, and of amusements for his sister; and he honestly strove to make both ends meet. Before the first year of his employment in Somerset House was at an end, he began to have his gloves cleaned, for at that period it was still considered necessary for young men to wear gloves at theatres and evening parties. In August, when people went out of town and the senior clerks were taking their holidays, he climbed up to the roof of an omnibus for the first time in his London life. It cost him a struggle, but Somerset House was a long way from his bright little apartments near Kensington Gardens, and it was better to sit on an omnibus than to walk both ways. He was pleased to find that no one had noticed him, and attributed the circumstance to the absence of most of his fashionable friends. But the habit, once acquired, was comparatively easy to keep up, and Ronald was much gratified to find what a material saving in his budget was effected by the complete suppression of hansom cabs. The next step, consequent on a formidable bill from his tailor, was to substitute dark trousers for the light and ephemeral garments he had hitherto worn. Metaphorically, he kept continually patting himself on the back for these sacrifices, and they appeared to him sufficiently great and noble to warrant a continuance of the daily flower in his button-hole.

Fortunately for a young man of Ronald's easy disposition, he had an innate aversion to anything low, nasty, and ugly. Probably his early years under the bright skies of Italy, certainly the loftiness of his mother's character, had had their share in imbuing him with aspirations which were thoroughly honest, if not ambitious; with thoughts which were pure, if they were not noble; and manners gentle and graceful, even if occasionally negligent. Thus he avoided the meaner vices into which young men, left to their own resources in London, are so likely to fall. He refused to share in those frequent 'nips' and 'pegs' which, then as now, were the curse of the young generation. He refused not only out of regard for his pocket and his health, but also because he detested alcohol. Therefore there was no special credit due to him for his temperance. As to the flirtations with barmaids and other ladies of humble extraction and doubtful *h*'s, which occupied a good many spare hours of his fellow-clerks' time, these had no attractions for Ronald. He often told his friends, laughingly, that Nature had denied him the great gift of making himself agreeable to barmaids.

'You should practise, old man. You'll get on all right by-and-by,' was the answer ; but Ronald did not wish to practise. The conversation of these young ladies appeared to him to be entirely devoid of the charm which he, perhaps foolishly and vainly, sought for in all women. He could never become accustomed to their style of chaff, nor did he see the points of the repartees which would often convulse everyone present with laughter.

Ronald felt that if these were types of the fair sex, he must needs become a misogynist. But he had access to so many houses, and was so kindly received by so many ladies of all ages, that he had no occasion to compete for the smiles of barmaids or ballet-girls. Though distinctly a detrimental, he was made welcome; for, notwithstanding the assertions of novelists and writers in society papers, there are many families where a gentlemanly young man of good manners is graciously and kindly received, even if he be neither a millionaire nor the heir to a title.

Ronald's conversation with his mother was a somewhat cynical summary of two slight and scarcely serious attempts he had made to 'settle in life.' Sensitive as he was to ridicule, he was always the first to laugh at himself, and thus take the sting out of a laugh against him. But Mrs. Lascelles was not at all inclined to laugh at her son's account of his misadventures, nor to agree with him in his own low estimate of his matrimonial chances. It is said that no man is a hero to his valet, but it may be stated with greater truth that every young man is a hero to his mother. Mrs. Lascelles believed implicitly in her son's abilities, which were no doubt excellent, if not brilliant. She thought his looks and manners irresistible, while they were only pleasing. She had absolute faith in his industry, and attributed his ill-success to every cause but the right one—his want of perseverance. But she was a shrewd woman, and was not blind to the dangers which beset a young man of Ronald's easy temper. The more fascinating he was, the more likely was he, in her opinion, to fascinate or be fascinated by a person quite unfit to become his wife.

Mrs. Lascelles had a mortal terror of 'entanglements.' She had spent so many years of her life in Italy, had heard so much scandal, and seen so much wretchedness without scandal, caused by ill-assorted marriages and irregular attachments, that she was in a constant state of anxiety lest her son should, somehow, fall a prey to an undesirable person, or become fettered by chains not sanctioned by the Church and society. Looking at him as she did through beautifying spectacles, she had a sort of indistinct idea that every other woman must also consider her son the handsomest, cleverest, and most attractive of young men. Put into words, she would, of course, have repudiated the suggestion; yet an idea of the sort was undoubtedly at the bottom of her fears and anxieties.

During the first two years Ronald resolutely stuck to the office on every working day from very few minutes after ten till the stroke of four, and, as bank-holidays were not then invented, he found the continuous attendance irksome enough, though it could scarcely be termed hard work by any except his mother and sisters. But when the third year of Somerset House drudgery opened, and the very welcome and liberal rise of twenty pounds in salary came as a matter of course, his patience began to give out. Ronald yearned to get away from London, from the unceasing noise of the traffic, from the dirty crowds, from the black dust and unæsthetic slums he passed through daily. Possibly his growing desire for freedom might have brought his Civil Service career to a premature end if great news from Portino had not reconciled him to his desk for a few months longer. His elder sister, Clara, only two years younger than himself, had charmed an English stockbroker who was spending a winter in Italy, seeing sights and collecting pictures, after ten years of unceasing work in Capel Court. Mr. Stent, wrote his father, was in every respect unexceptionable. Inquiries made through their old friends, Woodall and Co., Bankers, satisfied Mr. Lascelles that his daughter's suitor had, as he termed it in his consular language, 'a perfectly clean bill of health.' His standing in the City was unimpeachable, and no one had ever whispered a word against his character. Mr. Stent was about six-and-thirty years of age, and, as Mrs. Lascelles was careful to tell her son, he looked thoroughly like a gentleman, though he was not exactly handsome. He was very good to Clara, and did not ask for sixpence with her. So everyone was satisfied, and Ronald was informed that, as the wedding would take place early in May, he must be sure to obtain at least three weeks' leave about that time. Mr. Stent would shortly return to London to take a house and make final arrangements; no doubt he would call on Ronald, and the young man was instructed to be as friendly as possible to his future brother-in-law.

Not long after Ronald had despatched congratulatory letters to every member of his family, he received a neat, square envelope, directed in a commercial round hand. The note it contained was signed 'George Stent,' and was exactly the sort of note a man should write to another some years his junior, whose sister he is about to marry. There was in it no assumption of premature familiarity; no friendliness which might appear excessive before the two had met. It began as it ought to begin, 'Dear Mr. Lascelles.' It went on as follows: 'No doubt you have heard from Portino that your good and charming sister has promised to become my wife. I should be extremely glad to have an early opportunity of making the acquaintance of one with whom I shall soon be so nearly connected, particularly as your most estimable father and your dear mother speak of you with a pride which is, no doubt, entirely justified. I should do myself the honour of calling on you at your office, but pressure of work prevents my ever leaving the City during the day. To avoid postponing the pleasure of seeing you, I take the liberty of asking you to honour

me by your company at dinner on Tuesday next, at
the Franchise Club, at half-past seven.'

Although this letter was unexceptionable in every
respect, there was something in it which grated on
Ronald's nerves.

'D——n the fellow's cheek!' he exclaimed aloud ;
'fancy daring to call the dear old governor "estimable."'

Then he read the note again, and liked it still less.
Mr. Stent was evidently kind enough to patronize
him. His father and mother had, as usual, praised
him far more than he deserved, and so this man talked
of their pride in him as 'being, no doubt, entirely
justified.'

He handed the letter to St. Clair, his most intimate
friend, with whom he 'chummed,' and whose room he
shared at Somerset House.

St. Clair said :

'Well, it's all right. You'll go, of course. No doubt

you'll get a thundering good dinner. My brother-in-law treated me like a king before he was married, and when he comes up to town now he still behaves like a brick, just as if Dora might turn him off at a week's notice if he dared to be unkind to her little brother.'

When Ronald pointed out the offensive expressions, his friend pooh-poohed him.

'Nonsense,' he cried. 'This man's something in the City. These fellows have more to do than we have, and can't spend hours spelling over a letter. He just wrote what came into his head. Don't go splitting hairs, old chap.'

So Ronald accepted the invitation, though by no means convinced, and wrote as briefly as he could consistently with good manners.

CHAPTER III.

THE STENT CLAN.

Mr. George Stent was a man of most unattractive appearance. So, at any rate, thought Ronald. His future brother-in-law looked older than his years. His face was long and yellowish, his nose was obtrusive, his mouth large, and his dark hair sparse. He wore whiskers only, according to the fashion of reputable City men twenty years ago. His grey eyes were large, but not quite pleasant. There was a fishy stare about them which at first rather disconcerted observant strangers.

During the first half-hour Ronald wondered a

dozen times how his sister Clara could have accepted such a very unprepossessing person. For Clara was pretty and accomplished, had a charming little figure of her own, and had been courted and made much of by every man in Portino, whether English or Italian, ever since she had been sixteen. But by the time the *entrée* was removed (the dinner was a *tête-à-tête*) Ronald began to soften, and before the dessert was placed on the table he caught himself thinking that George Stent was rather a good fellow after all. For the stockbroker had spoken pleasantly of Mr. and Mrs. Lascelles, and enthusiastically of his betrothed, without boring his guest by dwelling too long on his affection for her. He seemed to take a kindly interest in everything and all that concerned the family, and even talked of the English cricket club at Portino, and its prospects, as if he knew all about the place. Then by an easy transition he turned to pictures, and listened to Ronald's views on Italian art

—from cinque cento to the present time—with apparent deference and attention.

Ronald was agreeably disappointed, and reproached himself with having judged too hastily. This fellow was certainly ugly, but he was cultivated and good natured. He must be what is termed a good 'all-round man.' Sententious perhaps, and with manners of which the extreme courtesy bordered on formality. But though Ronald himself generally erred on the other side, he always much admired the old style, and was ready to be pleased by a person who never for a moment appeared to forget what was due to a gentleman dining with him.

After dinner Mr. Stent's younger brother appeared with a friend of his, and the party became more intimate and merrier. As the eldest among them, and the host, George never entirely forgot his courtliness nor his gravity, but he unbent, smiled kindly at the stories told, condescended to tell a few little artistic anecdotes himself, and delicately closed the entertainment long before the young men had ceased to be amused.

The progress of the engagement was as smooth as its beginning had been auspicious. Mr. Stent was lavish in valuable presents to his bride and tasteful gifts to every member of her family, and even to her school friends. He dashed off to Italy, not so easily reached from London as it is now, at the cost of five days and nights' travelling, merely to spend a few hours at Portino. He occasionally asked Ronald to dinner, frequently consulted him about future arrangements, and even carried him off to Hancock's to help him in the choice of jewellery. In short, everything was exactly as it should be. The only trouble was that political events at that time made it impossible for Mr. Lascelles to leave his post. Stent had been anxious that the whole family should come to England for two or three months, and that the wedding should take place in London. But this proved impossible. The war with Austria was over, but matters were still very unsettled, and the whole of Italy was disturbed. It was not a proper time for a family to travel, and it was not a time at which the English interests at Portino could be intrusted to a young and inexperienced Vice-Consul. So, in May, the wedding took place at the Consulate, the bridegroom's family being represented by his two brothers only.

Ronald spent a very pleasant holiday, and renewed his acquaintance with the friends of his boyhood, now grown up to be young men and young ladies. For three weeks the quiet Consulate was lively with preparations for the great event, with the great event itself, and with festivities hastily got up to console Clara's friends for her departure. There were numerous little 'dancing teas,' though the season was far advanced. There was a two-days' picnic to the Certosa. There were sailing trips on the quiet blue waters of the Mediterranean. There was a cricket-match between the rival clubs of Portino and Camporeale, in which Ronald, the champion Portino bowler, took seven of his opponents' wickets for twenty runs, to his own glory and his friends' satisfaction. In fact, they had a good time all round. Even Mrs. Lascelles joined in the fun and, in the prospects of the future, forgot the sorrow which a mother must always feel when parting with her daughter.

Mrs. Lascelles loved her daughter as a matter of course, but her heart was not wrapped up in Clara. Of her three children, Ronald had always been the one who monopolized her affection. Even while her head and hands were busy for Clara, her heart went out to her son, whose welfare and interests were supreme with her. She even went so far as to speak to George Stent about his future, and to hint very delicately that possibly the wealthy stockbroker might 'do something for him' some day. Her gentle insinuations were received with the deferential courtesy Mr. Stent always displayed to his future mother-in-law, and even before the honeymoon was over Mrs. Lascelles had a convincing proof that they had fallen on fertile soil.

For the City man made a proposal which showed extraordinary affection for his wife and for his wife's relations. He wrote to suggest that as long as Ronald could not find anything better than the Revenue Office he should take up his quarters with them, where he could have two comfortable rooms in their new house, a large and commodious one, near Hyde Park. Of course he should be quite his own master; but it would be a positive boon to Clara to have her brother living with her. He, Stent, was much engaged in the City, and could seldom return home before seven. At first Clara would find it very dull if she were quite alone. Now Ronald's office hours being much shorter, he would be able to take his sister out occasionally, join her afternoon tea, and keep her from moping by home associations. Mr. Stent added that in such a house as his the presence of an additional member of the family would make no appreciable difference, therefore, of course, Ronald would be saved the entire expense of his present lodgings.

This offer was made after Ronald had returned to London, but Mr. Stent sent it to Mr. Lascelles at Portino, instead of first informing the young man of his hospitable intentions. Perhaps he had anticipated that Ronald would receive it with less warmth than his father and mother. At any rate, it was sent to Somerset House at once in a very enthusiastic letter from Mrs. Lascelles, and a scarcely less appreciative one from the Consul. The offer was most kind and thoughtful. The plan would save Ronald over a hundred a year, and in his anxiety that his son should accept the offer, Mr. Lascelles voluntarily added that he would reduce the allowance only by forty pounds—

the exact sum Ronald spent in rent. He added that, of course, both he and Mrs. Lascelles had at once written to their son-in-law to accept his kindness on behalf of Ronald. The ground, therefore, was cut from under his feet.

Ronald did not wish to go to Porchester Terrace, and, if unfettered, would have declined the invitation at once and decisively, although he knew that the saving of even forty pounds a year would be a considerable relief to his father. He had been entirely free for several years, had gone out and come home when he pleased, had not been accountable to anyone for his hours, or for the disposal of himself and his time, and he was sure that the change, even to his sister's house, would prove very irksome.

And he much disliked the idea of leaving his friend, St. Clair, with whom he had lived on excellent friendly terms for so long. He had not learnt to love his brother-in-law, although he would have been at a loss to give any better reason for not liking him than the very vague assertion 'that he was a bore.' Therefore, when Ronald had received his letter, and had thought the matter over a little, he hoped that St. Clair would express such a disgust at the proposed arrangement as to afford him a good excuse for declining it. He was horribly disgusted when his friend, after reading the letter which Ronald handed to him, simply remarked :

' It is a capital idea ! How very jolly ! Fancy being saved Mrs. Western's bills, and having better atten- dance than those stupid girls who never stop a week after they have learnt their business !'

' But what will *you* do, old man ?' asked Ronald aghast.

' Oh ! I shall get on well enough. Anyhow,' he added mysteriously, ' probably we should have had to make a change soon. I shall be devilish glad to get away from Mrs. Western's. We'll give her notice to-night.'

Ronald saw his last chance of escape disappear. He had to give in, and four weeks later was installed at his sister's, where he had two small, but very well furnished, rooms allotted to him on the second-floor. Everything was exactly as it should be, and he could find nothing whatever to grumble at. On the first evening, when Clara left the two men over their wine, Mr. Stent addressed Ronald with his usual solemn courtesy.

'I hope you will be comfortable, Ronald, and will liven Clara up. She seems rather dull, poor girl.'

'I will do what I can,' said Ronald.

'No doubt, no doubt! But, of course, I can't expect you to be always at your sister's beck and call. She does not expect it herself. You will be going to your club occasionally, and meeting your friends, and in the winter you will be full of invitations again. You must make yourself at home. So here is a latch-key. But mind you are careful to put up the chain and bolt the door when you come in, and don't make more noise than you can help.'

Mr. Stent solemnly handed the latch-key over the table. As Ronald grasped it, he added impressively :

' And, Ronald, I am to some extent responsible for you; I hope you will not abuse this key.'

The young man stared, and then laughed.

' Abuse it ? Responsible ? I don't see what you mean. I will be careful to shut the place up, and I won't admit burglars, if that is what you are driving at, George.'

' That is not exactly what I was " driving at," as you term it,' replied Mr. Stent, with a thin smile. ' However, I believe it is all right.'

' Why the deuce should it not be all right ? exclaimed Ronald. ' Bless you, I have had a latch-key for the last ten years.'

' I dare say, I dare say,' answered Stent. ' But of course you will have to be more careful in your sister's house.' He emphasized *sister* to place Ronald at his ease.

'More careful?' repeated Ronald. 'I don't habitually come home drunk, old man! I shan't tumble on the stairs and upset the furniture more than once a week. And of course Clara knows my ways, and she won't mind having me kick up a bit of a row between times. I'll always be in before the milk; the servants won't know!'

'Ronald!' exclaimed Mr. Stent, seeing that he was being chaffed, a process he detested.

'Don't be frightened, George,' said the young man, not quite good-naturedly. 'Clara shan't be put out, nor you either.'

Mr. Stent subsided, not satisfied, but obliged to look as if he were. Then he went on:

'By-the-by, you may smoke in your sitting-room. I have had double doors fitted, so that none should come into the rest of the house: only don't smoke on the stairs, please.'

'I won't,' replied Ronald. 'Thank you for thinking of my habits.'

'Why, yes,' said Stent. 'I only smoke after dinner myself, but then you have more time. Will you come into my study, and have a cigar now?'

The latch-key did not prove dangerous. Ronald saw very little of his brother-in-law. He was off to the City before nine; and when Clara found out that her brother hated the eight o'clock breakfast, she established one which was not put on the table till her husband had gone. Then Ronald often dined at his club, and more frequently Clara and George dined and spent the evening with some member of the Stent family, which was very numerous and very clannish. So Ronald did not find it as irksome as he expected, and the winter passed uneventfully, as did the following season.

It was some eighteen months after Ronald had taken up his residence at Porchester Terrace that a change came. The birth of a son and heir was expected, and the house had to be turned upside down. Mr. Stent seemed to fancy that the arrival of this baby was an historical event of the utmost importance. To hear him, one would have supposed that no baby had ever been born before.

Ronald rejoiced at an excuse for leaving his sister's house. There were, said he, too many Stents about. He could not always shut himself up in his room, nor could he be uncivil to his brother-in-law's family. But the people were utterly uncongenial to him, and certainly unlike any of his own relations and friends at Portino.

Full of their own affairs, busy with each other's families, and overflowing with brotherly, sisterly, and cousinly affection to each other, these good people seemed to live in a world of their own which was certainly not the big world, and equally certainly not Ronald's world.

Anything that fell in with their views and opinions was right; everything else was wrong, and even shocking. If a Stent took up a book and praised it, the whole clan of Stents were full of admiration for the work. If a Stent thought little of an artist, that unfortunate painter was at once put down as an impostor and a humbug by every member of the family. It was 'great news,' and all the Stent carriages were ordered out to impart it to the ladies' friends, and to enable them to talk it over, if William Stent took a house in the country for six weeks. If Frederick R. Stent's wife gave her cook notice, she at once drove out to tell Mary Stent, and Miss Eliza Stent, and Mrs. W. Stent. Then they would all meet at George Stent's house, and discuss the matter at full length during the whole evening.

When the baby was expected, the whole Stent clan was in a state of perpetual agitation. Every female relative thought it necessary to call at least thrice a

4—2

week, and to stop two hours, to keep 'poor Clara's spirits up.' In such a case it was absolutely necessary, they said, that the lady should not be dull, nor alone.

The Saturday evening dinners at the house of Stent senior, where the whole clan assembled, were converted into a royal court for Clara's benefit. When she drove up, a gang would rush out to help her into the morning-room—for, out of deference to her condition, Mrs. Stent senior had changed the venue from the first-floor to the ground-floor. There would almost be a quarrel as to which was the most comfortable seat for her. Old Mr. Stent would take her in to dinner (though she was the youngest of his daughters-in-law) with an exaggerated show of care, as if she had been a piece of antique Venetian glass. The whole dinner-table was excited until a stool had been placed under her feet.

In the middle of the repast, some over-anxious member of the family would call out, in a loud voice:

'Are you *sure* that you are quite comfortable, Clara dear?' and, ten minutes later, Mrs. Stent (senior) would interrupt the flow of conversation by the inquiry, 'Don't you feel it too hot, Clara?' and then whisper significantly to any chance stranger who might, unfortunately for himself, have been invited to the Stent family dinner.

The ladies would retire very soon 'so that poor Clara might not be fatigued,' as they were careful to say, audibly; and when they reached the drawing-room, poor Clara, who would have liked to play the piano or do anything else lively, would be gently supported up to a bedroom to 'lie down and rest.'

If Ronald by chance met a Stent in the street, whether a distant cousin or a brother of George's, he would at once jump down the young man's throat with the anxious inquiry: 'How is your dear sister? One ought to be very careful, you know.'

The Stents being a very large family, Ronald was

always meeting one or the other, and he began to think that he had better put a scroll round his hat, with the words ' My sister is very well, thank you.'

The young men of the Stent clan never ran into debt ; and the daughters of that ilk never flirted. There was not room in the old-established firm of Stent and Cowcroft for all the youths of the name, but other openings were found for them in the City. When a young Stent attained the age of ten, he was, as a matter of course, sent to a certain private school on the South coast, where Stents had been birched in old times long past, and where Stents now acquired all that it was necessary to learn at school. At seventeen or eighteen, it was considered proper for a Stent to ' go to the university,' as it was termed in the family. This did not mean that either Oxford or Cambridge would be favoured by the matriculation of so promising an *alumnus*. Time was too valuable for a waste of three years at so critical a period of a young man's life. The founder of the clan had been one of the early supporters of the London University, when that institution had been established, and his descendants were not likely to forget their duties by deserting the Gower Street College, which is, in the minds of most persons, always confounded with the examining and degree-conferring body at Burlington House. So a year, perhaps two, were profitably spent in wearing a cap and gown, and attending lectures. There was great joy in the family if one of its members, by a fluke, obtained a sixth certificate in junior mathematics, and on such an occasion, the winner of Academic honours could not be sufficiently fêted, nor warned earnestly enough not to work too hard. When this ordeal was over—for no Stent had ever been known to take a degree—a convenient stool was found for the youth within two hundred yards of the Bank of England. At Stent and Cowcroft's, it was a matter of course that there should be at least two young men of the family learning the business, and being educated to become partners ; but their progress was not confined to their own firm. They invariably got on in the City. When our George Stent, Clara's husband, had been three years with a good financial house, its senior partner had occasion to remark that the young man had never been late at the office, except once, when he was in a train which broke down ; that he had never missed a single working day; and that he had never made a mistake in the quotations of the market. With such regularity and such industry, no man could fail to get on ; and very few years later, George Stent and a cousin were started in business on their own account by the clan, which furnished the necessary funds as a matter of course. Stent Brothers—as the new firm was styled with a view to the future—never opened speculative accounts ; never bought or sold without ample margin ; never lent money except on unexceptionable security; and would have been stricken with paralysis, if anyone had suggested that they might possibly sometimes have a flutter on their own account. So they made less than many of their competitors; but they never lost anything. They always went on making money, not spending a quarter of their income, and steadily laying by for a rainy day.

Thus it happened that when George Stent married Clara, he was a very 'warm' man, and could well afford to take her without any dower. It was a strange and unusual thing for a Stent to marry a penniless girl and there had been some little surprise expressed in the camp when the news came. But when the marriage was once accepted, Clara was welcomed as warmly as if she had had millions; and they were all so pleased with her, that in the exuberance of his pleasure, her father-in-law said to her encouragingly, 'My dear child, you will soon be quite a Stent.'

The young girls of the family were equally praise-
worthy in their conduct. They were taught all the
proper accomplishments by a certain Miss Dawson,
who being now nearly fifty, had instructed successive
families of young female Stents ever since she had
commenced her career as an instructress at the age
of eighteen. If, unfortunately, the families of two
brothers, or two cousins, were both in want of a
governess, an arrangement was made by which the
little girls of one family went to the house of the
other from ten, say, till four, so that they might not
be exposed to the risk of having a new governess.
At eighteen a lady Stent was brought out, and presented to Her Majesty as soon as possible. Generally
about three or four years later there would be a little
whispering at the family gatherings, and confidential
views would be exchanged between the mothers in
Stent, while the men nudged each other and smiled.
These symptoms were well known. In less than a

fortnight, one fine day the Stent carriage would be driving about to all the various houses occupied by members of the family, a Stent coachman would be conversing affably with the various footmen, and two tired Stent horses would wish that they had died before that auspicious day. For Eliza Stent was engaged to young Green, of Black, Green, French-grey and Co., Throgmorton Street.

Above all things the clan disliked eccentricity. Their tastes, they said, were simple. George, John, and William for the boys; Eliza, Jane, and Mary for the girls, were the names they most affected. They were all supposed to be fond of music and pictures; and, indeed, they understood both sufficiently to talk about them with a great air of intelligence. Stent senior bought pictures; the younger members purchased water-colours and etchings. Every Stent was expected to go abroad for six months at least before his education was considered complete. This six months' tour was talked of by the clan for years before, and until some other member's turn came. George had voluntarily postponed his holiday till he had made a great deal of money, and it was then that he fell a victim to Clara Lascelles.

Of course, Ronald only gradually discovered the beautiful ways and simple customs of the family which had so innocently taken him to its bosom. When it began to dawn on him that George Stent was very much like William Stent, and that there was no great difference in conversation and ways between these two and James Stent, and when he also found out that James, William, or John, or two of them with their wives, or all of them, frequently dined at Porchester Terrace, and as frequently expected George and Clara to dine with them, he began to be affected by his usual complaint—boredom. When further he was delicately informed that, under penalty of being considered a brute, he was 'expected' to be at home when James, William, or John came to dinner, and to accompany George and Clara when they dined with Mrs. James, Mrs. William, or Mrs. John, his complaint assumed an acute form.

Fortunately the joyful event now expected gave him an excuse to leave which he was not slow to take. In vain his brother-in-law assured him that he would not be in the way, and that his room would not be required. He preferred leaving, and he did so all the more willingly that he had obtained three months' leave from his duties, of which he resolved to spend a greater portion at Portino. Here we found him discussing the future with Mrs. Lascelles.

CHAPTER IV.

TO LOVE OR NOT TO LOVE?

YES, Edith Woodall was a very delightful girl. There could be no doubt of her intelligence, which was apparent in every glance of her eyes, nor of her good heart, which was abundantly proved by the affection entertained for her by all who knew her, and by her numerous acts of thoughtful kindness which could not remain a secret in the small English colony of Portino. Yet, did Ronald love her? If love were really the passion described by poets and novelists, if its symptoms were always the same or similar, if the diagnosis of the disease as laid down by those who ought to know, were correct, then Ronald was not in love with her. He did not feel miserable if obliged to spend a few days without seeing her. He did not count with impatience the minutes which had to elapse before meeting her again. He could scramble along very comfortably for a week, or even longer, without any particular yearning for her sweet presence. He did not dream of her, still less did he lie awake thinking of her. He could enjoy himself very much at a cricket-match, or sailing, without her image disturbing his mind in the least. He could even get on very well with other young ladies, perhaps less intelligent and less kind-hearted, but yet quite delightful company. They did not suffer by comparison with Edith. Miss A. or Miss B., to whom he did not think of proposing, whom he did not care two straws about, were very fair substitutes for Edith if she did not happen to be in the way. He would talk to them, dance with them, and even flirt with them. When at last he was once more in the presence of

Miss Woodall, he did not feel any extraordinarily violent pleasure. He was very happy no doubt, but not so very much happier—was he at all happier?—than on the previous evening with Miss A. or Miss B. Of course she was their superior. He could talk to her on matters which would have been Greek to them —on books and art, and even politics, which were beyond their understanding. So he ran less chance of being bored by her, and Ronald was very easily bored. But he never remembered to have been bored for one instant by Edith Woodall. Perhaps that was a proof of love. Perhaps he, Ronald, was only capable of negative symptoms; not, in fact, a good subject for the complaint. Certainly he had attained the age of twenty-seven without having suffered any of the agonies described by poets and novelists—except for a short time. He had been much taken up by Miss Monsell, the beautiful American. He had thought her lovely, original, and delightful. When she gave him the cold shoulder, he had been 'awfully hard hit,' as he termed it, and had moped for a couple of weeks. But now, thinking over his feelings after a year's interval, he believed that he had suffered from mortified vanity rather than disappointed love. He knew that he had made a favourable impression on the girl, and fancied that that favourable impression had gradually deepened into a stronger feeling. He thought himself indispensable to her happiness, and he built beautiful castles in the air. Suddenly she showed unmistakably that Mr. Ronald Lascelles was not at all indispensable to her, and his beautiful castles collapsed. He had been horribly disappointed and annoyed, but was he heart-broken? Not quite—at any rate not then. Possibly he had no heart to break, that is, no sensitive heart such as lovers are supposed to possess. Now, comparing his feelings about Edith Woodall with those he had entertained for Miss Monsell, the American heiress, he found them very dissimilar. There were great differences, no mere shades of distinction. The American was dashing, peculiar, and original; she would never condescend to obey, though she might possibly consult her husband if she loved him. With her Ronald felt that she would absorb him altogether, that he would probably always play second fiddle to her lead. But then her personality imposed itself in such a way that he foresaw no unpleasantness in thus dropping into the second place. The case was obviously very different with Edith Woodall. Brought up in a quiet family circle, having spent the greater part of her life in Portino, she spoke Italian and French like a native, but was absolutely ignorant of the pursuits and amusements in which young ladies like Miss Caulfield and Miss Monsell had spent half their life. She knew nothing of the fashionable world of London; she had never been on a race-course; she had never ridden anything more lively than a brown Italian donkey: she considered it a great thing to go to half a dozen dances during the winter. Of course she knew much which the other young ladies did not know; in culture she was obviously their superior, in temper, as Ronald expressed it, 'she could give them fifty in a hundred.'

So though he thought that he was not quite as fond of Edith as he had ever been of Miss Monsell, he was attracted to her by totally different qualities. She would undoubtedly be a thoroughly good wife to any man she loved. She was an excellent house-keeper, too, which was no unimportant matter, as Ronald well knew, having had to 'chum' it for some years with a bachelor friend. Probably she would make a thousand a year go as far as two thousand in other hands. She had taken charge of her widowed father's house when she was sixteen, and had proved an excellent hostess. Their entertainments were, no doubt, simple and homely, yet the

5—2

one English banker in Portino, which was full of strangers every winter, received many people at his house, and there was scarcely an evening during the season on which the family were quite alone.

But was not this catalogue of virtues almost commercial by its very completeness? Surely a fond lover could not thus glibly run off the moral perfections of his mistress, and calmly compare them with the charms of other women! A lover, thought Ronald, would be more enthusiastic and less sensible. Love is, of course, traditionally blind. Now he could see too well that Edith's mouth was large, and her nose neither aquiline and Roman nor straight and Greek. He could also perceive that she had no large quantity of hair, though what there was of it was fair and soft. If he were in love with her, he ought to consider her mouth exactly the right size, to be convinced that the ancients were fools in their opinion about noses, and, in fact, to be under the impression that her face and form were perfection.

He had heard his friends speak about the ladies of their hearts, and they had done so with an enthusiasm which, unfortunately, he did not at present feel. His 'chum,' St. Clair, had some time ago fallen in love with a certain Miss Denny, whom he had met in Suffolk, where he was invited to shoot. When he returned to Somerset House he could talk of no one but this lovely Miss Denny. She was beautiful, she was brilliant, she was the jolliest and dearest girl ever seen. Her figure was perfection, and as to her face, so pretty and *piquante*, it was too delicious to describe. As the autumn wore on into the winter, St. Clair's enthusiasm rather increased than diminished, and Ronald had become very curious to see this wonderful Miss Denny, who had fascinated his good-looking friend. At last the Suffolk folks came up to town for the season, and one afternoon St. Clair carried Ronald off to be introduced to them.

Miss Denny turned out to be a small, skinny little thing, with nothing attractive at all. She was quick and bright, and dressed well ; but Ronald was entirely at a loss to understand how his friend, a man who went about quite as much as himself, and had had ample opportunities of seeing the prettiest women in London, could consider this young lady at all good-looking. Yes, love, or at any rate St. Clair's love, was evidently quite blind—utterly unconscious of any imperfections in the lady ; wrapped up in admiration for her as if she were the only woman in the world, looking at her through spectacles which rounded off angles, filled up hollows, straightened ugly curves, and curved ugly straight lines, enlarged that which was too small, and diminished what was too large. Were such glasses always the accompaniment of love ? Could love not exist except with blindness ? Or was this all-admiring, all-beautifying temper only confined to St. Clair? No, for Count Stornello, one of the young Italians who was most intimate with the English colony at Portino, had confided to Claude his enthusiastic admiration for Signora Ferraris.

Signora Ferraris was married, but of course in Italy it is quite permissible for young men to proclaim their love for somebody else's wife from the house-tops, and the last person to take offence is the husband. Stornello was more demonstrative than St. Clair, and equally blind. Mdme. Ferraris was fat, and had no complexion at all except what she borrowed from the little pots on her toilet-table, and she was nearly old enough to be the Count's mother. But he raved of her wonderful eyes, which indeed she knew how to use to the best advantage; her faded complexion was to him attractive *morbidezza;* her ample form became the rounded contours of graceful matronhood. Stornello would call on her, and wait an hour for a kind glance; he would look at his watch a hundred times during the afternoon, hoping for the moment when she would drive across the Via Marina, and give him a suave bow or a coquettish nod; he would rush to the theatre the moment the doors were opened and never take his eyes off her box till she entered it, when he could often not wait for the *entr'acte*, but must push out through the crowd to wait on her. All this was indeed now over, but Ronald remembered it well.

At these absurdities Ronald had often smiled. How he envied St. Clair and Stornello their illusions! How wonderful a creature Edith Woodall would appear to him if he could only borrow their glasses! For she was young and graceful, and had none of these shocking defects so painfully apparent in Miss Denny and Signora Ferraris. But he had not lost his ordinary eyesight, and instead of rhapsodizing like Stornello, or unceasingly talking of his love like St.

Clair, here he was calmly making a schedule of her good points and bad ones, as if Miss Woodall were a horse offered for sale. So much was clear, he had not, like so many others, allowed his heart to control his reason or his eyes. So he returned to the idea which had already run in his mind. Perhaps, after all, he was incapable of the foolish and blind passion to which other men were subject. Perhaps he was not made to suffer the tortures nor to enjoy the infinite pleasures of an all-absorbing love.

No doubt they would be very happy together if she accepted him, which he thought probable though not certain.

But still Ronald had misgivings. Having almost made up his mind to propose, on the ground that he loved Edith as dearly as he was ever likely to love any-body, he suddenly began to consider the matter from the lady's standpoint. After all, was it quite fair to offer her what professed to be his hand and heart when the heart was really not entirely hers? Was it just to a girl so charming and so thoroughly straightforward, to come to her under false pretences? She certainly deserved a more ardent love than he could bestow, a warmer lover than he would become. If, as he occasionally thought, she cared more for him than he did for her, if she loved him sufficiently to accept him, it would surely be an ill reward for her devotion to give her mere friendship. But Ronald was not so conceited as to be quite sure of the love which his mother thought was undoubtedly his. In fact he looked upon matters far too dispassionately to be sanguine about anything. He was not sure of Edith's feelings, and he was still more uncertain about Mr. Woodall's views. To do him justice, the prospect of a share in the Bank and of the affluence which would follow, scarcely influenced him at all. He could not at present afford to marry a penniless girl, but then he was not bound to marry immediately.

He could wait till his position improved. He must work for his living, and by-and-by, perhaps, he would have earned a competence and could look out for a wife without regard to her worldly means. Ronald would certainly not marry some one he did not care about, for the mere sake of wealth and position. To sell himself, to owe all to a wife whom he did not love, was a thought too horrible to contemplate; and he knew well that, anxious as his mother was to see him comfortably settled, desirous as was his father for his worldly prosperity, neither parent would urge on him a distasteful match.

CHAPTER V.

TWO BEFORE AND TWO AFTER.

'HAVE you thought that matter over, Ronald?' said Mrs. Lascelles the next morning, when Mr. Lascelles had gone into his office, and Teresina was practising noisily rather than melodiously in what was formerly the school-room.

'Yes, mother, and I cannot make up my mind,' replied Ronald.

'Don't you like her after all?' asked Mrs. Lascelles.

'I do like her very much, but I cannot make up my mind that I love her enough to want to marry her.'

A look of anxiety passed over Mrs. Lascelles' face. She rose from her chair, and approached her son, placing a hand on his shoulder.

'Ronald, is there anybody else?' she asked, fixing her eyes on his face with a look of grave inquiry.

'Oh no, mother dear,' he replied, more lightly than she quite liked.

'No one at all? are you quite sure?' she repeated. 'No lady of whom you are fond? Tell me frankly, my dear boy. If you have some engagement, some fancy which you would rather not tell your father ——'

'Nothing of the sort, mother,' interrupted Ronald; 'nothing, upon my honour!'

Mrs. Lascelles kissed him warmly. 'I am so glad,' she said, resuming her seat, while a look of pleasure returned to her eyes. 'You would tell me if there were, would you not? I would not scold you, child; I know young men are often foolish without being really wicked.'

'I would tell you anything, mother dear,' answered Ronald, kissing her in turn; 'even if I had done something to be ashamed of. But fortunately I am quite free.'

'Then what can be your objection to Edith Woodall?' asked Mrs. Lascelles, returning to her text.

'I have no objection to her at all,' said Ronald. 'I have told you the only reason why I cannot make up my mind to propose to her.'

'Nonsense, Ronald; you mean that you don't adore her as if she were a goddess, and are not silly about her! I think you are much more likely to be happy together than if your head were full of absurd ideas about impossible perfection. She will make a most excellent wife, and I am quite sure the ridiculous love-making one sometimes sees is quite sickening, and is no proof of real affection at all.'

'But surely I ought to love the girl whom I marry?' objected Ronald.

'Love! of course you should love her. As a matter of fact, I believe you do; at any rate, quite enough for the present. If you are so lucky as to get her to say yes, you will adore her before you have been married a week. According to your standard I was never in love with your father, nor did he ever go down on his knees and worship me.'

. Now this might be true, or it might not; Mrs. Lascelles certainly intended to tell the truth, but old people sometimes forget what their feelings were thirty years before. Whether she had passionately loved her husband or not, Mrs. Lascelles had been a devoted wife; and though in early days surrounded by good-looking Italians whose sole pursuit seemed to be to pay her compliments and to make love to her if she permitted it, she had never had the shadow of a flirtation, and had accepted all the pretty things she heard as so much rubbish which might amuse her, but could not divert her thoughts for a moment from the husband to whom she trusted implicitly, and who had the same faith in her. There had been troubles in their early married life, but these troubles were financial and political only. Never had the gloom of doubt nor the darkness of jealousy been cast over their path. They were perfectly happy with each other, though happy in a quiet subdued manner which might appear cold to some persons. Ronald had never thought about his parents' married life for the simple reason that there was nothing to make his thoughts wander into that channel. They had always got on very well together, though he heard his father occasionally grumble, and his mother would sometimes say, 'Oh, how fidgety you are to-day, dear!' But that was the nearest approach to a quarrel that had ever taken place in his presence; and even this was an event of rare occurrence. Now, however, that his mother cited her case as an example of how happy people could be together without any show of passionate adoration, he began to doubt whether his parents' married life was quite the ideal he dreamt of. The thought seemed unfilial and almost profane, but was their affection not rather commonplace and dull?

'Of course your experience should guide me, mother, he replied affectionately, sitting down at her feet; 'but I must confess I am rather nervous about it.'

'Shy?' inquired Mrs. Lascelles; 'surely not?'

'No. Not shy about speaking to Edith, I don't mean that; but nervous about the result of the experiment. You see we can't get unmarried again if we should not suit each other.'

'Trust me, my dear' replied his mother. 'When you have been married six months to so sweet a girl as Edith Woodall, you will wonder how on earth you ever managed to live without her!'

Ronald laughed.

'It is nothing to laugh at,' continued she; 'it is quite true. And now I have lost Clara it would make me very happy to have another daughter to love. You could not bring me one whom I could love better than Edith.'

Mrs. Lascelles spoke rather sadly; Clara had at one time been quite in sympathy with her mother, but her letters now showed her to be becoming more and more a member of the Stent family. They told of new dresses, and grand dinners, and household details; but Mrs. Lascelles did not find in them that confidential interchange of ideas and hopes, of thoughts which she believed she had a right to expect.

Teresina was still very young, and her mother missed the eldest daughter more than she cared to confess even to herself. There was, therefore, a tiny spice of very pardonable selfishness in the advice she was giving her son.

'You seem so very sure of the matter, mother,' said Ronald. 'You don't seem quite to understand me. We are not all made alike, you know.'

Mrs. Lascelles looked up inquiringly, ' Is there anything new to understand ? It appears to me plain and straightforward enough. Here is a nice girl who I believe is ready to marry you, and who I know would make you thoroughly happy. She has money, too, which is an additional advantage, and the only objection you raise, having no attachment elsewhere, is that you are afraid you will not love her well enough. My dear boy, I am quite satisfied that your scruples are exaggerated and mistaken. You will make her an excellent husband, and you will be as happy as the day is long. If you don't say anything to-day, at any rate you should speak to her at Cavaliere Donati's to-morrow ; you must not delay too much, for I can tell you that Edith Woodall is much admired, and will not remain unmarried long.'

Still Ronald was not quite satisfied. There was no one more competent to advise him than his mother, and he ought to have been satisfied, but he was not.

He spent the evening at home, and was very happy
with his sister and his sister's friends. They talked
and played at table-turning, and had a little music,
and were altogether a jovial little party. When old
Marietta came to fetch her young mistress, Mrs.
Lascelles gave Ronald a meaning look. It was
perversity on his part not to understand it, but he
pretended to be deep in a conversation with Signora
Boticelli, the mother of one of the girls. He did not
wish to walk home with Edith; he might be tempted
to say something he would afterwards regret. He
would like another night to think it over.

But when Teresina innocently said, 'Ronald, surely
you are going to see Edith home,' as if she had been
egged on by Mrs. Lascelles, there was no excuse
handy. A glance of pleasure flashed across Edith's
face, but she protested. It was quite unnecessary;
Marietta could take care of her well enough; the
Tramontana was so cold, and so on. But of course

Ronald insisted on escorting her, and having donned his overcoat, offered her his arm when they reached the streets. Such a thing was not usual in Portino, where Italian customs, so strict in some respects and so lax in others, had overridden their English habits. Ronald would not have been surprised if she had refused the support, for in Portino if a girl walked up the Via Marina on a young man's arm, they were at once supposed to be engaged. So he rather lightly and maliciously resolved to consider her response to his offer as a test of her feelings towards him. If she declined, he would not risk a more important request; if she accepted, it should mean that she would accept his hand as well. Of course the test was not a fair one, for poor Edith could not guess what was passing in his mind, and might very well have refused to give late wayfarers in Portino an opportunity for gossip. Ronald himself was conscious of the absurdity of the ordeal, but nevertheless he stuck out his arm in a determined manner. And his heart beat faster than usual as he did so. There was a moment's hesitation ; Edith looked up at him doubtfully. After all, thought Ronald, my mother was wrong. But then the little hand was placed gently on the rough coat, and Ronald could not help feeling gratified. It is always pleasant to think that an attractive girl likes you, even if you are not prepared to marry her on the spot. The distance to Casa Woodall was far too short for much conversation. But it led along the broad Via Marina, past the brightly lighted *façade* of the Casino Nobile. As they approached the door of this building, two young men emerged, and met them rather abruptly. After a short stare of surprise one of them made a most elaborate bow to Miss Woodall, and both of them of course stepped aside. Edith returned the bow, which made Ronald ask her whether she knew the man.

'It is the Marchese della Rocca,' replied she. 'He

brought letters to papa, and is stopping here for a little while; I believe he is a friend of the Donatis, too.'

'Then I suppose he will be at their dance to-morrow?'

'Oh yes, of course. He has asked me for a dance already.'

'Indeed,' said Ronald, displeased, though he scarcely knew why, save that the short glance he had had of the Marchese had not produced a pleasant impression. 'Will you keep a couple of dances for me, Miss Woodall?' he added, after a moment's interval.

'Certainly, if you wish,' replied the girl, with alacrity.

This made Ronald bolder. 'Two before supper and two after?' he suggested.

'Is not that rather too many?' asked Edith, smiling.

'No, not half enough!' he exclaimed, as they reached the banker's door.

'Will you come in?' inquired Edith; 'I am sure papa is still up.'

Ronald declined. He was not going to disturb Mr. Woodall at eleven o'clock. But as he took leave under the *porte cochère,* he said : 'Mind, two dances before supper and two afterwards ; I will be there early, and will ask nobody till I have seen your card.'

'That will be very unkind to the other girls,' said Edith.

'They must get on without me till you come,' he replied, laughing ; 'I dare say they will do very well. Good-night, Miss Woodall. 'Mind,' he added, holding her little hand longer than was quite necessary, 'it is a promise.'

'It shall be, if you like. Good-night, and thank you so much for bringing me home.'

CHAPTER VI.

A VERY GOOD BALL.

THE dance at the Donatis' was to be the last of the
Portino season, and their large rooms were quite fitted
to give a crowning finish to a lively winter. Italian
palazzi are not comfortable for a small family when
the Tramontana blows, and English people then sigh
for a snug little home in a London street; but when a
hundred people meet, and more than half of them
want to dance, the advantages are all on the side of the
vast rooms and the scanty furniture. Everybody worth
knowing in Portino was invited, and as there was no
competing assembly, nearly everybody came. Ronald
arrived early, escorting his mother and Teresina, in

whose favour an exception was made on this occasion, as she was not what we call 'out.' Father and son, having made their bows, walked through the rooms together.

'Do you know anything of that man, father?' asked Ronald, pointing out to the Consul the Marchese della Rocca, who, with his opera-hat under his arm, was bowing deeply to Signora Donati.

'I believe he is a very distinguished young man,' replied Mr. Lascelles. 'He is one of *the* Della Roccas, the old Tuscan family, you know. They have enormous property near Sienna.'

'What brings him to Portino, I wonder?' said Ronald.

'That is more that I can tell you, my boy,' replied the Consul. 'Probably he is merely amusing himself, like most of these young Italians. I understand that he is the chief of the eldest branch, and very well off indeed. His father died last year.'

'He is a beast, anyhow,' remarked Ronald.

'I don't see it,' replied Mr. Lascelles; 'I think he's very good-looking.'

But Ronald stuck to his opinion. No doubt the Marchese's appearance seemed to challenge public taste. His face was undoubtedly handsome—according to a certain standard. He had fine large black eyes, a formidable moustache twisted up at the points, a small straight nose, and a well-cut chin. But the way in which the man spoke and moved, nay, the mere shape of his collar was, in Ronald's opinion, sufficient for any well-regulated English gentleman to wish to kick him downstairs. *He* sniffed what his father was too old, or too Italian, to notice—the vainglorious air of the foreign lady-killer, than which nothing more offensive has ever existed. Della Rocca's low forehead was just high enough to contain mean thoughts behind it, and no more.

Ronald well knew the class of which this was a

superfine type; knew them too well. To him, born
and bred as he had been in Portino, these young
Italians had no secrets. Their bragging ways, their
shabby tricks, the coarseness of their feelings under
the gentlest manners, were familiar to him. Scarcely
two of the young members of the Casino Nobile but
had been guilty of acts which would have ensured
their expulsion from English society—scarce one whose
life would have borne even superficial examination by
an English father. To be known for having broken
women's hearts, and to have won large sums at cards,
was the summit of their ambition; to break these
hearts and to win money were the objects of their
lives. Nothing that was not punishable by law was
dishonourable; and many crimes of the penal code
were venial if undetected. To lie was no disgrace,
though to be found out and publicly accused of a lie
was cause for a duel. Yet these very men, men who
never read anything except the daily political rag,

men who spent their time in smoking and gambling or making false love, had polished ways, enchanting voices, and an ease of manner which most Englishmen could envy, without being able to imitate. They did not wash except, once in a way, for a ball, or in very hot weather, but they *looked* clean. They never washed away their vices, but they appeared virtuous.

The Marchese had more money than most of them, and as he spent it freely he was popular among men of his age. But he strove not for popularity among men, but for the love of women, and he looked like it. To Ronald he appeared as if 'liar' and 'seducer' had been written in black letters on his white, smooth forehead. His dress alone would have justified an assault. An enormous open collar, of which the corners were thrown back at a sharp angle, so as to display the throat, a waistcoat cut down extremely low, a gorgeously embroidered shirt-front with diamond studs, a whole bundle of miniature decorations in the button-hole of the satin-faced dress-coat. All seemed to say: 'Look what a fine fellow I am!' But then Ronald was cross, and he knew more of the Italian *jeunesse dorée* than most people, and possibly he made Della Rocca out to be a greater villain than the handsome young man really was.

At this moment Edith swept into the room with her father. Ronald hastily stepped forward, and was chagrined to see the Marchese seize the girl's card while he himself, as in duty bound, shook hands and exchanged a few words with Mr. Woodall. When at last he obtained the coveted bit of pasteboard, he noticed 'R' scribbled over it in too many places to please him. But there were several blanks, and four of them were soon filled by his own initials. Young Donati claimed Edith for the first dance, and then the Marchese came and swept her off.

She had certainly never looked better. Even the hideous crinoline of the period did not disfigure her.

Clad in white, with bouquets of real violets set round the top of her dress and catching up the ample gauze-like folds of her skirts, her fair shoulders seemed to gain by comparison with the tarletan. Her soft hair was full of golden flashes in the light of the candles, and her large dark eyes, deep with a pure maiden's thoughts, glanced quickly and kindly from one to another of her friends as she floated round the room to the seductive strains of 'Il Bacio.' Ronald thought that the way that Italian hound stooped over her, till his long moustache swept her soft cheek, was positively disgusting. And she appeared to him almost beautiful. That she was the best dressed girl in the room was certain, and he began to believe that she was one of the prettiest.

The waltz was at last over. Ronald rushed up and claimed the next, nor would he leave her side, forcing the Italian at last to walk off with a suave bow.

'What a lovely bouquet!' exclaimed Ronald, as

Edith smelt the violets and white roses she held in her hand.

'Yes, is it not?' said the girl. 'The Marchese sent it this afternoon. It suits my dress exactly. After all, there is no place like dear old Portino for flowers.'

'D——n the Marchese!' exclaimed Ronald, under his breath. 'Do you like that beast?' he asked aloud.

'Which beast?' inquired Edith, surprised, and looking round, as if she expected to see an ape or a cat in the room.

'Della Rocca, of course,' answered he.

'What language, Mr. Lascelles! Why do you call him a beast? I think he is very nice, and he dances beautifully.'

'I call him a beast because I know the sort of fellow,' answered Ronald.

'You seem to judge very quickly,' replied Edith.

'Yes; quickly, but justly. *You* cannot, of course,

know. Young ladies are not expected to know, but he is the last man I would like my sister to dance with.'

Miss Woodall looked much surprised, and Ronald had scarcely uttered the words before he repented. It was a mean trick thus to slander a man of whom he knew nothing unfavourable, and he was ashamed of himself directly. Just then the music began. In a pause of the polka he returned to the subject.

'I spoke hastily about Della Rocca just now, Miss Woodall; I really know nothing whatever against him. But the fact is, I hate him because he admires you. That is the long and short of it, and I may as well confess at once.'

Edith blushed a little, but answered lightly:

'Then you won't have many people to hate, Mr. Lascelles.'

'Della Rocca, at all events,' he replied. 'Why, he cannot take his eyes off you! Look at him now.'

'Shall we go on?' asked Edith, to get away from the subject which could not be agreeable to her, for while she was not able to pretend to dislike the fascinating Marchese, who had made himself very pleasant during their short acquaintance, she did not wish to quarrel over him with her old friend and ally Ronald.

So they again dashed into the dance. Edith understood the polka better than most English girls. With her it was not two hops forward with a kick, two hops back again with another kick, and then several hops round with more kicks. When she and Ronald danced it, the polka became as smooth and graceful as the waltz, with far greater variety. Without getting out of time they could swing slowly and talk, or twist easily and with no apparent effort through a crowd of hoppers, whose heels threatened at every moment to come down heavily and sharply on the toes of other dancers. Or, when there was room, they could glide swiftly backwards across the smooth parquet, or fly in swift gyrations round the fringe of the dowagers and wallflowers.

Della Rocca watched them intently, but there was no frown visible on *his* face as there was on Ronald's when he, in turn, had to watch the Italian leading Miss Woodall through the then fashionable lancers. The Marchese talked much to his partner in that low rich voice so often heard in Italy. There was an air of confiding secrecy about him even when he made the most commonplace remark. He spoke, too, with his expressive eyes, which now flashed in fun, then again cast tender glances, but were always turned in admiration towards Edith. She seemed to be amused and interested, and to listen to the handsome Italian with increasing attention. Not once did Ronald catch her eyes straying to where he was leaning moodily against a pillar. He could see her well from where he stood, and whenever the maze of the lancers cut off a full view for a moment, he could still distinguish her fair head bending towards the Marchese, and harkening to his honeyed words.

It was a bad quarter of an hour for Ronald, because he was beset with doubts and anxieties. He told himself that he was not jealous. He would not have minded it a bit if Donati or young Wells had started a mild flirtation with Miss Woodall; but it galled him bitterly that she should listen to this abominable creature, to this Marchese, whose very thoughts were hideous and revolting, whose very touch was defiling, whose soft speech and gentle manners were only a veneer which covered a cold and rotten heart. *He* could see through that thin coat of veneer; how strange that neither Edith nor his own father, nor hers, could perceive anything dangerous in the fascinations of the handsome youth. If he had decided to ask Edith to become his wife it would be a very different matter. Then he would see his way.

He could even now take the first opportunity to propose, and if she said yes, he would make use of his rights
at once, while if she refused him he would leave her
to the Marchese's wiles.

Should he do so ? Should he speak out during the
next dance, which was to be his ? Even yet, stimulated
as he was by his dislike of Della Rocca, he could not
make up his mind to the final plunge. He knew
himself too well to trust his impulse. He argued
with himself that he was irritated, cross, and even
jealous, and therefore in no fit condition to take so
important a step. Then the dance was over and he
saw the Marchese lead his partner into the tea-room.
He found her there ten minutes later, sitting in the
embrasure of a window, half concealed by the curtains.
She was toying with her fan and looking down, while
the Italian was whispering soft nonsense in her ear;
and his bold gaze was fixed on her fair face, and
striving to catch a glance from her averted eyes.

Ronald exercised all the self-control of which he was capable, and walked very composedly up to the couple.

'I beg your pardon, Miss Woodall,' he said calmly; 'I think this is my waltz. They are just beginning.'

Edith started, and dropped her fan, which the Italian picked up and handed to her with a sigh.

'I am utterly desolated,' he whispered, loud enough for Ronald to hear, 'to have to resign that beautiful hand. From heaven I descend to purgatory. But the tortures of purgatory are not eternal, you know. You will be the kind angel to raise me once more, will you not, *carissima signorina ?*'

Then he rose quietly, made her a dignified bow, and moved away, not deigning even to look at Ronald.

The latter now spoke in the usual ball-room tones of easy *persiflage*, resolutely beating down his anger at what he termed the Italian's impertinence.

'You are really flirting dreadfully with the Marchese!' he said, as Edith took his arm.

'Am I?' she asked innocently. 'I really did not know it.'

'Why, you knew he was making love to you most audaciously!' exclaimed Ronald. 'He called you his angel and his dearest!'

'Did he?' again inquired Edith rather maliciously. 'I dare say.'

'Well? and you listened to it all quietly, and took it in quite easily, as if you liked it.'

'Oh!' she replied; 'all Italians talk a great deal of nonsense. They think themselves bound to say absurd things to every girl they dance with.'

'Do they *all* talk like the Marchese?' inquired Ronald.

'Some of them. Not quite all, perhaps. I am quite used to it, and it goes in at one ear and out at the other. But they are very amusing and nice, and the Marchese dances beautifully.'

In the intervals of the valse Ronald returned to the charge.

'You do not attach much importance to the romantic declarations of Della Rocca?' he asked.

'Certainly not. That style is usual here. It's more amusing, though, than to have a partner who can only talk about the weather, like some of papa's English friends.'

'I admit that,' answered Ronald. 'It is more amusing, but more dangerous.'

'Dangerous? I don't think so,' said Edith. 'I know how to take care of myself, Mr. Lascelles.'

'Are you quite sure? You see, Miss Woodall, I should not mind if I were quite certain that you took all these compliments and enthusiastic declarations for what they are worth. But I am afraid you believe half of them.'

'That is not a particularly civil speech,' remarked Edith. 'You don't think I am worthy of them, then?' she asked archly.

'Worthy!' exclaimed Ronald; 'you are far too good for any of these wretches. It is because I think so much of you that I bore you with my warnings.'

'There is your prejudice again,' said Edith, holding up her finger.

'No, indeed, no prejudice. But will you give me the supper dance, Miss Woodall? This has been such a short one, because I did not find you till it was nearly half over,' Ronald asked hastily, for young Donati was approaching to claim his partner, and she would be hurried away in a moment.

Edith gave him her card. There was an 'R' very distinctly and largely writ at the line corresponding to the supper dance. Ronald very deliberately drew out his pencil, scratched out the 'R,' and wrote 'Lascelles' in the blackest characters over it.

'Thank you, Miss Woodall,' he said, returning the card.

Then he went off to dance with Miss Donati, and afterwards gave Teresina a turn, as he termed it. But he was careful to be close to Edith at the end of the quadrille which preceded the supper dance, and hardly had the music ceased when he claimed her from Mr. Paull, a mild young Englishman who was travelling in Italy with his tutor.

In a minute the Marchese came up to the couple, who were walking up and down the *salon*, waiting for the music to begin. He accosted Edith with his usual deep bow:

'Signorina,' he said, 'I think that you were so gracious as to promise me the pleasure.'

'Thank you, Marchese; I am engaged.'

'Yes, signorina, to your devoted slave,' said Della Rocca, bowing again, without appearing to notice Ronald.

'Signorina Woodall has promised me this dance,' said the latter.

The Marchese still did not look at him, but turned again, appealing to Edith.

' Mr. Lascelles' name is down, I believe,' she said, handing her card to Della Rocca.

The latter glanced at it, and then returned it with another deep bow :

'Pardon me, signorina; I have made a mistake. What would you ? The wish is often father to the thought. A thousand excuses, I pray.'

And he retired. But this time he shot one look of deep meaning at Ronald, who caught himself blushing violently.

' After all, I think I must have been engaged to the Marchese,' said Edith, looking at her card carefully after they had taken a few turns round the room. ' Mr. Lascelles, you scratched his name out !'

' I did,' said Ronald quietly.

'How dared you?' asked Edith, but not by any means as if she were much vexed.

'Simply because I wanted to dance with you myself, and take you in to supper.'

'How did you know that I should permit such a thing?' she inquired. 'Now you must take me to the Marchese at once, and I will apologize. He is in the corner there.'

'Indeed you will do no such thing,' replied Ronald. 'Is it such a great sacrifice then? Have you been deprived of a very great pleasure?'

'Nonsense!' she answered. 'But it was very rude of me.'

'The rudeness was not yours, since you knew nothing about it,' said Ronald. 'Now, let things alone, please do. What is the use of making such a fuss about it? Come, let us take one more turn.'

And Edith was whirled away, not unwillingly. She

did not really care one bit about dancing with Della Rocca, and much preferred having Ronald's comparatively prosaic talk to the Italian's flowery and exaggerated compliments. Though she pretended to attribute Ronald's warnings entirely to prejudice, she was herself dimly conscious that some of the Marchese's speeches were not quite such as he ought to address to a young unmarried lady.

Too pure herself to know anything of evil, yet, her perceptions being awakened by Ronald's hatred of the Italian, she had noticed something in his tone and manner which was disagreeable, and some mysterious meaning seemed to lurk in his honeyed words and soft smiles, which she was absolutely disinclined to fathom. So, on the whole, she was by no means sorry not to have the Marchese's company during the supper interval, which, at the Palazzo Donati, was no brief pause between the dances. The Donatis prided themselves on doing things well, *all' Inglese*, and the supper was a very different affair to the weak tea and cakes usual at Portino dances.

There was room for everyone to sit down at the little tables set out in the great hall, which was one of the features of the palace. A numerous array of liveried servants brought what was required; there was no squeezing and hustling, nor urgent demands for champagne and pressing requests for the leg of a fowl. Young Donati, with Teresina on his arm, saw Ronald and Edith looking for a table.

'Come with us, caro Rinaldo,' he exclaimed; 'here in this corner. I have a charming *posto* reserved for us.'

They agreed willingly, and there was a merry little *partie carrée* in that distant corner. They were all on excellent terms with each other, and even had they been inclined to be dull, which they were not, Teresina's intense delight at this her first ball, would have kept them going. The Marchese was invisible, and Ronald, having forgotten his doubts and worries, was as merry as any of them. It was some time before they broke up, and, as a matter of course, Ronald led off his unresisting partner to the after-supper waltz, always the best of the evening.

Edith had lost her card, not perhaps without a little assistance from Ronald, who had slyly removed it from the supper-table, and torn it into small pieces. At any rate, Miss Woodall knew not to whom she was engaged, and danced away with Ronald as if cards had never been invented. The Marchese did not come near her. Donati frankly volunteered to give up the next galop in favour of Ronald, if Teresina would dance with him instead; and as the little maid was nothing loth, the exchange was effected.

Soon, too soon, Mrs. Lascelles rustled up to warn them that it was time to depart. Mr. Woodall, too, appeared from the card-room, and casually mentioned that it was past three o'clock. Teresina was the most unwilling to go, but at last the three ladies descended the wide stairs to the cloak-room. Ronald fetched his overcoat, and waited for them in the hall. At that moment the Marchese stepped up to him, dangling one glove in his hand in a nonchalant way:

'A thousand pardons, signore,' he said very gently; ' permit me to ask you a question.'

'Go ahead,' said Ronald, surprised.

'Excuse me again,' continued Della Rocca, 'but may I congratulate the charming Signorina Edit?

'What about?' asked Ronald gruffly.

'About her betrothal to you, signore. You, of course, are still more to be congratulated. That is understood. But not having until now the honour of your acquaintance, I would wish to present my homages and most respectful good wishes to the lovely bride.'

'What do you mean? I am not engaged to Miss Woodall,' answered Ronald sharply.

'Then, signore,' said the Italian, in a grave tone, 'you must understand that I cannot allow my name on a lady's card to be erased by a stranger. Consider yourself *souffleté*, if you please.'

And with these words he raised his hand and lightly passed the glove across Ronald's face. Several young men were about, and they sprang forward hastily. Ronald lifted his arm to knock Della Rocca down, when it was seized by Stornello.

'Don't make a row here!' he whispered quickly, for just then the ladies came out of the cloak-room. 'See the women into the carriage, and we will talk presently.'

Ronald had flushed scarlet, and restrained himself with the greatest difficulty. At that moment Donati rushed downstairs to bid the ladies farewell, and in his impetuosity almost knocked the two young men over.

'A thousand pardons!' he said. 'Caro Rinaldo, I

nearly upset you. I was hurrying to make my re-
verence to your charming mother and sister.'

The youth's blundering helped Ronald and Stornello over the awkward moment. The ladies were
helped into the carriage, and he told Mrs. Lascelles
that he would walk home and smoke a cigar. The
Marchese was one of the group under the *porte
cochère*, and bowed deferentially to Edith as she
stepped into her father's brougham. When it had
rolled away Stornello turned to Ronald.

'You are among us here in Italy, my friend, and
you must fight.'

'Of course I'll fight!' exclaimed Ronald. 'I'll give
that blackguard a jolly good hiding. Let us get out
and set to at once.'

'I'm afraid this will hardly do,' whispered he. 'You
have been grossly insulted before all these men '—and
indeed a group round the Marchese were talking fast
to each other, gesticulating and looking towards

Ronald—'and you must fight a duel *en règle*, if you do not wish to be disgraced in Portino.'

'All right,' answered Ronald. 'Go and tell him so. Anything you please, as long as I can give the fellow a lesson.'

Count Stornello stepped towards the group, bowing. The men fell back at once, so that he could approach the Marchese della Rocca, who was leaning against a pillar twisting a cigarette.

'Marchese,' he said, 'I have had the honour of meeting you at the Club. I am Count Stornello.'

Della Rocca inclined his head slightly.

'You have insulted my friend, Signor Rinaldo Lascelles, and he demands satisfaction.'

'*Gia*,' murmured Della Rocca, again bowing.

'Will you give me the name of some gentleman who will arrange preliminaries?' asked the Count.

'The Signor Guarini will do everything that is

8—2

required,' said the Marchese, pointing to a military looking man of about thirty.

Signor Guarini bowed, and Della Rocca slowly passed out at the *porte cochère*, saying:

'A rivedere, signori. I shall wait for you at the Club.'

CHAPTER VII.

THE CASINO NOBILE.

ALL this had not passed without attracting a certain amount of attention. Several men had witnessed the insult, and some had joined the group under the entrance as the ball drew near its end. Count Stornello, who was a young man of Ronald's age, and had not lived in Italy all his life without several 'affairs of honour,' was equal to the occasion.

'Signori,' he began in a clear but subdued voice, 'let us all go away at once. This unfortunate discussion must be concluded without any scandal, which would be most annoying to our hospitable friends here.'

There was a murmur of approbation.

'Signor Lascelles and the Marchese della Rocca will have had a dispute over cards at the Casino. *E inteso ?*'

There was another murmur of assent.

' And,' he went on, 'all of you being *galant' uomini*, the authorities will know nothing of this business until it is over.'

He then took Ronald's arm and walked out.

' We must find another second,' he said, when they were alone. ' I should like someone rather more experienced than myself. Of whom could you think ?'

It was difficult to think of anyone at the moment, and yet both were very unwilling to postpone matters.

' You cannot fight till Saturday, at any rate,' remarked the Count. It was already Friday morning.

' I should like to go and fight now,' said Ronald.

' That is out of the question, friend. People do not go out direct from a ball unless the offence is a mortal one.'

'So it is,' exclaimed Ronald hotly.

'Pooh! nonsense. The glove did not hurt. You will soon wipe that insult out, and teach the Marquis better manners. I think on the whole it will now be best for us to go to the Club for ten minutes, so as to give colour to the story about a quarrel at cards. You would not like Miss Woodall's name mixed up with this affair, would you?'

'Indeed not,' replied Ronald; 'not for worlds.'

'Then come along. I will arrange it.'

It was not as easy to arrange as the Count had supposed. Della Rocca did not seem to care about the young lady's name being kept out of the affair. In truth, he would have desired it to be proclaimed loudly that he was fighting for the blue eyes of Signorina Edit. But pressure was put on him by Guarini and other members of the Club, and, after much mysterious whispering in corners, a little card-party was arranged in one of the private rooms. It was

painful to Ronald to have to expose himself to a
second insult, even though it might only be a piece
of acting. He sat down to *écarté*, with the Count at
his elbow to prompt him, while Guarini and Carda-
villa supported the Marchese. Della Rocca paid no
attention at all to the cards, while Ronald was far too
excited to distinguish hearts from diamonds.

'Mark three,' whispered Stornello to Ronald. He
did so. When the cards were next dealt he turned
up a king and made the trick.

'Game!' said Ronald.

'Excuse me, signore,' observed Della Rocca. 'You
made the trick, and marked the king. That is two.'

'Well,' observed Ronald, obedient to his friend's
whisper. 'And three before makes game.'

'You had only two points before!' exclaimed the
Marchese.

'It is a lie,' shouted Ronald, forgetting his part,
and determined that the first insult should not come
from his adversary this time.

In a second he had the cards thrown into his face by the Marchese, and there was a tremendous noise, all jumping to their feet and talking at once.

'You fool,' hissed the Count into Ronald's ear. 'Now he is the insulted party, and may claim the choice of weapons.'

'For goodness sake let this farce come to an end,' replied the young man, impatiently. 'I don't care what I chastise him with. A stick is good enough for me.'

'Patience, patience!' said the Italian. 'Now go home quietly, and I will come and see you in the morning. Mind you get to sleep at once!'

Ronald squeezed the proffered hand, and obeyed without a word. He lighted a cigar at the door almost mechanically, and slowly walked towards home in a sort of dream. Was he asleep, or had he taken too much wine? Was all this reality? Should he have to meet another man in deadly combat within the next few hours? In a moment something had happened which might cut off his life on its threshold, or be the cause of taking away that of a man no older than himself. It was too strange, too surprising to be real; it must all be an illusion! Yet he still felt the hot blood rise to his face when he thought of Della Rocca's glove, so it must be real after all. It had all taken place in a very short time. When he reached the Consulate he could still see a light in his mother's room. He threw off his overcoat, and his eyes fell on a white rose, still full of perfume though half-faded. It was one Edith had given him out of her bouquet during the after-supper dance.

'Poor child,' he thought. 'If she had suspected that my scratching that brute's name out would lead to this, I should not have persuaded her so easily to stick to me. She is a dear, nice girl! I wish I loved her, I dearly wish it. But pah! I must not get sentimental.'

He took the rose out of his button-hole, once more inhaled its fragrance, full of sweet memories, and placed it carefully in his pocket-book. Then he obeyed Stornello's orders by going to bed. He was quite sure he could not sleep, for the events of the evening had been too exciting. But he was mistaken. In a very few minutes he calmed down, for after all, thought he, nearly every one of these Italians he despised so much had had at least one duel, and they were none the worse. Besides, he had as good a chance of killing as of being killed, and though he did not like to contemplate what his after-life would be if he cut short that of the Marchese, yet his hatred of him was so great that he dropped off into a dreamless sleep with his fists clenched.

Indistinct visions of ball-rooms, flowers, and small swords, young men with offensively low collars, and of a dark girl with a dazzling complexion and full lips, not a bit like Edith, flitted through his brain, but they scarcely disturbed him. The bright Italian sun was already high when he was roused by a knock at the door, to which he murmured the traditional '*Avanti !*'

It was Giuseppe, the 'odd man' at the Consulate, who cleaned boots and knives, ran errands, and did duty as Ronald's valet when he was at home.

Ronald sat up in bed. The man gave him a letter.

'It is urgent,' he said, 'or I would not have disturbed his Excellency.'

His Excellency rubbed his eyes, and the occurrences of the previous night came back to him. He seized the letter impatiently. It was from Count Stornello.

'Take breakfast quietly at home,' said his friend, 'as if nothing had happened. Come round to my lodgings at about eleven o'clock. We shall be undisturbed there, and I will tell you what we have settled. It is to be this evening if possible.'

It was now half-past nine, so there was no time to waste. Ronald rose hastily and inquired whether anybody was yet stirring. He was told that Mr.

Lascelles had rung his bell, and that the Consul would probably soon be in the dining-room. Here, indeed, Ronald found him, sipping his coffee and reading the newspaper—or, rather, the tiny Italian rag which did duty for a newspaper.

'Good morning, Ronald,' said he; 'I hardly expected you to be down so early, after dancing all night.'

'I was not so very late, father,' replied the young man. 'I came in very soon after you.'

'I know, I know,' answered Mr. Lascelles. 'But you see I was playing whist quietly all the evening, and you were dancing about the room with hardly a pause. You seem to have enjoyed yourself very much.'

'I danced a great deal, and the supper was excellent,' said Ronald.

'I should think so! The Donatis do everything very well. You don't seem to care about your breakfast, Ronald. Why, at your age I could dance all night and eat a beefsteak in the morning,' said the Consul, laying down his paper to look at his son.

His father's absolute ignorance of the events of the evening was reassuring to Ronald, who was nervously impatient to get away, for fear of betraying his excessive preoccupation. Mrs. Lascelles, who joined them soon afterwards, was clearly also without any suspicion of the *fracas*.

When Ronald rose to leave the room she kissed him with more than her usual tenderness, as if to show that she was pleased with his conduct. But she only asked :

' Shall you dine at home to-night, Ronald ?'

To-night ! Where would he be to-night at dinner-time ? Would he *be* at all ? Would there not, before then, be an end to his doubts and hesitations, to his hopes and fears ?

'I think so, mother,' he replied, 'if it is seven o'clock as usual.'

Then he went to Stornello's lodgings, modest, like those of most young Italians, who have very little idea of making themselves comfortable in luxurious chambers. Here he found his friend, and Colonel Martini, an elderly man, who had earned distinction and a severe wound in the late war, and had only just been invalided on a full pension.

'My dear Rinaldo,' said Stornello, 'you know Colonel Martini, of course? I felt that I had not sufficient experience in an affair of this seriousness. I have had a couple of little discussions myself, but they were not very important. So I asked the Colonel to help us.'

'But,' answered Ronald, who had often met Colonel Martini at the Consulate, 'my father——'

'Mr. Lascelles,' interrupted Martini, who was very fond of addressing Englishmen by English titles, and invariably directed his notes to Ronald's father, 'Mr. the English Consul Lascelles, Esquire,' 'I am an old friend of your respected father. He is an honourable gentleman of good blood, and has the heart of a soldier, and has served his country and risked his life for her more than once, though only a civil servant. I am sure the British Consul would approve of the course I am helping his son to take.'

And he held out his hand and pressed Ronald's warmly.

'But you will not tell him?' cried Ronald.

'No, my dear young friend. I will not tell him until all is happily over. For what should I make a loving father anxious? A duel cannot be avoided without disgrace. I am no advocate for duels, when the cause is trivial; but in this matter the insult was so gross and so public that I do not see how we can arrange matters without, at least, a wound, and we have acted accordingly.'

'I am glad to hear it,' replied Ronald. 'I would in any case have refused to arrange matters.'

'Young blood will be impetuous,' the Colonel went on. 'I am glad to see you have a spirit, as indeed your father's son could not fail to have. But it was my duty to arrange things amicably if I could. Therefore, when the good Count here called on me this morning very early, we went to Signor Guarini's house and demanded that the Marquis should make a public apology at the Casino.'

'Of course he refused,' interposed Count Stornello.

'Naturally!' observed the Colonel. 'I quite understand. The quarrel at the Club is not the real cause of the dispute. But you may trust me, young men,' and the old officer winked significantly. 'A lady's name must never be mentioned among noblemen.'

'So we are now waiting for the Marchese's seconds,' said Stornello. 'We have agreed that you are to fight at six to-night.　We do not dare to postpone the affair till to-morrow, because such a lot of fellows at the Club know of it, and the police would be sure to hear. The sooner it is settled the better.　Now what arms would you prefer, Rinaldo mio?　You are good at the *salle d'armes*, I know.'

'I should prefer swords,' answered Ronald, 'as I must not use my fists.'

'The Marchese della Rocca,' interposed the Colonel, 'is, I understand, a first-rate swordsman.　He is also a good shot.　Can you use the pistol, Mr. Lascelles?'

'I have practised a little, but I am not really good,' said Ronald.

'Then we must endeavour to obtain swords,' replied the soldier.　'This is, of course, your first affair?'

'Yes.'

'Then, above all, you must not be nervous.　The bravest man is nervous at his first duel till his blood gets warm. I was much frightened myself, and would have wished to run away. Now, what can we do to divert our young friend?' asked the Colonel, turning to Stornello.

'He must certainly not be alone. Could you get one of your comrades to accompany you to the shooting-gallery, just to practise a little, you know, without tiring yourself?'

'Oh yes!' replied Ronald. 'But I should prefer to go for a sail in the *Santa Lucia*. There is a nice breeze to-day, and no sea to speak of,' he added, as he looked across the room out of the window and noted the bright waters of the bay sparkling in the sunlight.

'My dear young friend!' exclaimed the Colonel in surprise, 'you might be sea-sick, and the motion of the boat would affect your steadiness. Not for worlds!'

Ronald laughed. 'I suggested it because I think

9—2

that the breeze would do me good, and blow away the cobwebs. I was up late last night, you know.'

'Better let him go!' said Stornello. 'And it will disarm suspicion.'

'Well, then, be off,' observed the Colonel, shrugging his shoulders. 'I shall never understand you Englishmen. But mind you are back by four o'clock at latest.'

'And,' added Stornello, 'you may as well have a suit of dark clothes sent here. Then you need not go home to dress.'

'All right,' exclaimed Ronald, quite pleased. 'Of course you will look after everything?'

'Of course,' answered the Colonel. 'Leave yourself in my hands. You could not easily find anyone,' he added, grasping Ronald's hand, 'who is more anxious for the honour and the safety of his old friend's son.'

CHAPTER VIII.

'SANTA LUCIA.'

AWAY sped Ronald to the quay, where he soon found Gasparo, the man in charge of the little yacht *Santa Lucia*, owned by the Consul, and which was now mostly used by his son whenever the young man was at Portino. Gasparo was ordered to uncover the sails and prepare to get under way; Ronald would come off in a shore-boat. He dashed into his own room to change his clothes, and in passing his sister's put his head in.

'Will you come for a sail, Teresina? Start in five minutes.'

And then he hustled Giuseppe off to get young

Donati to join them: For not only did he want to 'divert himself,' as the Colonel expressed it, but he was particularly anxious that all Portino should know of his trip, so that none should suspect what drama or tragedy was to follow it. By the time the brother and sister were ready, Giuseppe returned breathless to announce that the Cavaliere would meet them at the quay. Then they thought of provisions, and Mrs. Lascelles soon packed a little hamper with a couple of rolls, a bottle of *Barolo vecchio,* and some cold meat. No one would have suspected that the merriest of the jolly trio who pushed off to the *Santa Lucia* in a gaily painted wherry was, a few hours later, to fight a duel to the death with a practised adversary.

It was a pleasant day. The wind was still off the land, but its violence had quite abated. The sun was bright, and the sky cloudless. The *Santa Lucia* heeled over to the gentle breeze, and cleaved the waters of the Mediterranean with no more than a graceful bow to the little waves which lapped against her smooth sides. They sailed round the great Russian ironclad which was moored in the bay, and then crossed to Punto Sereno, where some of the wealthy Portinese spent the summer season. Here all the villas were shut up, and the bathing establishment was deserted. But they picked up a buoy in the tiny harbour, and ate their lunch on the deck of the *Santa Lucia*, watching the sea-gulls gather round the little bits of meat they threw overboard, and chatter and quarrel over them, till a big cormorant would sail in amongst them, and scattering the noisy crew, secure the morsel for himself. They bought some tiny oysters from a fisherman, and broke nails and knives in trying to open them. Then Teresina sang the sweet Neapolitan sailor-song:

'Sull' mare lucica
L' astro a' argento ; . . .'

and Gasparo, who was usually very shy about his vocal powers, at last consented to begin: 'Caroli-

netta,' accompanied of course with the charac-
teristic gestures and mobile changes of expression
which none but Italians can imitate, when, for the third
time, he trolled out:

> ' Com' è bella, quello riso!
> Com' è dolce, quello viso!
> Tutti cred' in paradiso
> Quando sto vicin' a te,'

with his great horny hand first on his mouth, then
on his eyes, and lastly on the place where his heart
was supposed to be. Ronald suddenly said:

'Thanks, Gasparo! But we must get home; it is
three o'clock. Let go the buoy and haul up the peak.
I will sail her back.'

'Why start so early, Ronald?' asked Teresina plain-
tively. 'We have lots of time before dinner, and it is
so awfully jolly.'

'I am very sorry, dear,' answered he. 'But I have
a most important business engagement at four, and
we have barely time to get across.'

Teresina pouted up her little mouth, and Donati looked quite heart-broken. But Ronald was firm, and soon the *Santa Lucia*, with the wind just abaft the beam and every sail drawing, was flying across the bay towards the lighthouse on the Portino mole.

What a peaceful, pleasant scene, yet how instinct with life! Would Ronald ever again be standing on the narrow white deck of the tiny *Santa Lucia*, steadying the tiller, and letting the heavenly breeze cool his forehead? Was this the last time he would see his pretty sister sitting against the lee bulwark— her lithe figure clad in soft blue serge, her brown hair straying from under the glazed sailor hat, while her bright eyes glanced mischievously at Gasparo, who, leaning against the mast, was finishing, with the help of a clasp-knife, the remains of the Padroni's luncheon? Would he never again behold Portino, with its white houses and green shutters, stretched along the blue bay, the sunny hills behind dotted

with villas, and the bright green of the orange-trees
and the dull grey of the olives? Should he never
more hear the chorus of the red-capped fishermen
as they hauled in their long drift-nets half a mile off
the mole:

<blockquote>
'Santa Luci—a
Santa—Lucia'?
</blockquote>

    *   *   *   *

The dinghy's keel grated on the stones. Donati
jumped out to help Teresina, who, disdaining assistance, skipped up the steps like a deer.

'Will you take Teresina home?' said Ronald to the
young Italian; 'I must look after my business. I
am late as it is,' he added, glancing at his watch,
which showed five minutes past the hour.

Donati was delighted.

'You will be sure to come to dinner, Ronald,' called
Teresina to him, as he hurried across the wide quay
towards Stornello's rooms. 'Thank you so much!
Such a jolly sail!'

As Ronald climbed up the steep stairs of the Casa Luigi, where his friend lived, he suddenly stopped. What a curious circumstance! He had spent the whole day without a thought of Edith! He had enjoyed the sail, though he knew what must follow. He had gently, if sadly, contemplated the possibility of never seeing his good father, his adored mother, or his dear little sister again. He had taken a good look at the beautiful bay, as if it were indeed to be the last look. He had listened to Gasparo's song, and to the fishermen's chorus, as if he would never hear them again. He had watched the sea-birds, and thought that the rustle of their wings and their hoarse shouts were like the cries and sighs of the shadows in that abode where the souls of good heretics and unbaptized children dwell.

Dante had come back to him as if he had but just risen from reading the sonorous stanzas. But he had not thought of the terrifying possibility of horrors;

only of the curious mystery of the endless future which he might know in a few hours.

But in all these wanderings not once had his mind strayed to Edith Woodall. Yet it might almost be said that he was about to risk his life for her.

Was that, then, love?

CHAPTER IX.

SAN CRISTOFORO.

THEY were waiting for him impatiently.

'These Englishmen take things very coolly,' said the Colonel, pulling out his watch.

'All the better,' replied Stornello. 'Less likely to be nervous.'

'Yes, but *che curiosa gente!* Now if one of us others had to fight a duel, we should first go and practise for a couple of hours at the shooting-gallery, and then have a jovial *déjeûner* with a large party of friends at some good restaurant. It keeps the spirits up, and prevents a fellow feeling dull.'

'That is what *I* did,' assented the Count.

'So did I when I still fought duels,' continued the Colonel. 'But this young Englishman goes off on his boat, on the rough stormy sea, and perhaps he is sea-sick; surely he has had nothing to eat, no company, no liveliness, no preparation! *Curiosa gente!* I only hope he has not been upset, or drowned perhaps. They would say he was afraid!'

Ronald was announced just as even Stornello was beginning to be seriously anxious. He apologized for being late; he had forgotten the time in the pleasure of the sail. Martini shrugged his shoulders, and Stornello showed him into his room to change his clothes.

The seconds superintended his *toilette*, which is a matter of serious importance on such an occasion. They told him that unfortunately, in the opinion of those best qualified to form one, the choice of weapons rested with Della Rocca; and he had of course selected pistols. Therefore the adversaries were to dress in dark clothes, with a frock-coat closely buttoned up. They were to meet at San Cristoforo, about five miles out of Portino, and the matter was to be settled in a little wood behind that village. A carriage had been ordered for five o'clock.

It appeared punctually to the minute. During the drive Ronald's friends attempted to cheer him. But as a matter of fact he did not feel particularly depressed. Somehow he had made up his mind that he would be shot through the heart, and his thoughts were busier with what would come afterwards than with the duel itself. It would be a pity to leave the world so soon, and every now and then a momentary sadness would come over him. It was a bright, beautiful world, and he had as yet seen so little of it! There was so much joy, so much brightness and light, for those who sought for them, and did not make themselves miserable by imaginary woes. A sigh escaped his lips as he remembered a sunny afternoon at Lord's,

and a strangely beautiful face under a quaint parasol.
But then again a smile stole over his face as he thought
of some pleasant dinner in London or an amusing
adventure at Portino; and he was not in the least
frightened.   When the Colonel whispered,

'Keep up your courage, my friend; keep steady, or
you will miss him altogether,' he stretched out his arm.

'Feel my hand.   Look at it,' he said.   'Does it
tremble?' and the old soldier was surprised at his
placidity.   It was the calmness of excessive nervous
strain; not that of practised valour.   The doubts of
the previous days, the fatigue of the ball, the quarrel,
and the excitement of the morning, had worn out his
nerves, which were simply quiescent for the time.   The
carriage drew up at a bridge outside the tiny hamlet
of San Cristoforo, and Colonel Martini led the way up
a path along the little brook which there crossed the
road.   Stornello followed, carrying a suspicious-looking
case covered by a cloak.   Ronald knew the place well.

In May, when the Spanish chestnuts were in bloom, and in June, it was a favourite spot for picnics and excursions.

At this time of the year the trees were bare of leaves, and only here and there a timid violet peeped out of the grass. For about a quarter of a mile they followed the water; then they turned to the left up a steep path, through an undergrowth of chestnuts which were cultivated for vine-sticks. The long stems grew so close together that, though the leaves were scarcely budding, the thicket was impenetrable to the eye beyond a few yards. After a short ascent, during which the Colonel repeatedly said: ' Gently, signori, gently! our friend must not be out of breath,' they reached an open glade where the ground was almost level. At one end of it was a huge chestnut-tree, whose majestic branches extended far across the young grass. At the other extremity was a quiet pool, whence flowed a tiny rivulet. The glade was closely surrounded by underwood, and the setting sun was shut out from it by the dense vegetation. Under the tree were three gentlemen, one of whom Ronald at once recognised as Della Rocca. By the pool were two more, one of them carrying another suspicious-looking case.

' Wait here,' whispered the Colonel to Ronald, and stepped forward with Stornello. All the men bowed to each other most ceremoniously, and Della Rocca's seconds, with Ronald's friends, stepped into the middle of the glade to consult. Two pistol-cases were produced, and the weapons compared. Then Colonel Martini came back to his principal, who was watching the proceedings intently, leaning on his thick orange stick.

' We have arranged to place you with your backs to each other at thirty paces,' said he. ' When you hear the word *Avanti*, you will turn round and, if you please, advance on your adversary ten paces, but not nearer. Or you may fire at once if you prefer it. He will also fire when he pleases. Some people rush forward and fire instantly; I do not advise this. Let me see you hold out your hand at full length.'

Ronald did so.

'It is well,' said the Colonel; 'you are a *bravo giovine*. It trembles not. Now recollect. When you turn round, do so quickly, covering your right side with the pistol arm, and keeping your body sideways towards the enemy. Do not forget this; it is more important than all other matters. Keep your eye and the barrel of your pistol fixed on him; and fire when you please. If you choose to advance, do so step by step carefully; place the right foot first, and bring the left slowly after it. Never lose your balance, nor,' added he, smiling, ' your head.'

'What do you advise about firing? Shall I step forward first, or stand where I am ?'

'Well, my dear young friend, it is a fearful responsibility to advise you in such a matter. For the Marchese is said to be a good shot, and if you wait for his fire, you might be incapable of returning it. With an ordinary marksman, I should certainly say, wait. For if you stand still he cannot get nearer than twenty paces, which is a long distance to hit; and then, when he has discharged his pistol, you can measure your ten paces forward in cool blood. But with Della Rocca I would not advise—I cannot—I dare not!'

'Very well,' said Ronald : 'I understand perfectly. Who are the other two gentlemen?'

'Doctors, *caro mio*—just as a matter of precaution. Not that they will be wanted, of course.'

Stornello now stepped up.

'Are you ready, Rinaldo?' he asked.

'Quite,' answered Ronald.

'Wait a minute!' cried the Colonel. 'Let us look at your dress. That coat must be buttoned up to the neck, and the shirt collar turned down. No white must be visible. That is right. Now, my friend, good courage, and God be with you !'

Stornello grasped his hand silently, and the two led him forward. There was not much to choose in the stations. A single ray of the horizontal sun pierced the thicket, and sent a broad band of yellow light across the grass about ten paces in front of the pool; otherwise the whole glade was in soft grey shadow. Stornello and Guarini drew lots for places. Guarini won, and elected to place his man near the chestnut-tree, which had the advantage of being a little higher than the other end. The distance was carefully measured by Martini and Della Rocca's other second; then the doctors retired to the edge of the brushwood, and the two adversaries were walked off with their backs to each other. The Colonel placed the pistol in Ronald's hand, and gave it a final clasp as he did so.

'Corragio,' he whispered. Then he went quickly to

the centre, for, as the oldest man present, he had been asked to give the signal.

' Are you ready, gentlemen ?' he asked loudly.

' Yes,' said Ronald in English.

' Pronto,' came from under the old chestnut.

Then, ' *Avanti, signori !*'

Ronald turned quickly, following instructions, and protecting his body with his arm, he aimed his pistol straight at Della Rocca. The latter moved swiftly forward. He took the ten paces in barely five seconds, but in that short time all Ronald's previous life seemed to come before him.

' God bless and preserve my mother and father !' he whispered, and then came a violent sharp pain in his right leg, as if a huge knife had been plunged into him. He scarcely heard the report which followed. He sank down on his knee, and saw that the doctors were rushing forward. But in a second he had regained his presence of mind. He waved them back with his left hand, and, by a tremendous effort of will, rose to his feet.

'A moment, signori!' he cried; 'it is merely a scratch.'

Then he slowly advanced the wounded leg, and again raised the barrel of his pistol. He watched Della Rocca. The young man was pale as death, almost livid. Even Ronald could see him tremble. He still stood guarding his body with his right arm, but his now useless pistol had fallen on the grass beside him. Four more paces, and Ronald reached the ray of sunlight. It lit up his brown hair, and cast a halo over his pale face. It glanced on the barrel of the pistol, and was reflected in his sparkling eyes. It showed a small, red stream trickling slowly down from his side on to the green grass. Then he stepped again into the shadow, his lips firmly set, his teeth clenched, and a look of sternness on his countenance which none had seen before. He carefully counted the ten paces, and then stopped, while the seconds were motionless with anxiety and horror. Very steadily and very slowly he raised his pistol till it covered his adversary between the eyes.

Della Rocca was shaking like an aspen; but the pistol followed his movements, and the gallant Don Juan of the previous evening, resplendent in huge collars, satin facings, and orders, now looked a very different object.   His partners would not have recognised their handsome admirer in that shrunken trembling figure.   The Marchese's eyes were fixed with a stony glare on the barrel, so near him now, and so fatally steady.   The Italian fancied that he could almost look down it.

'Now it is quite impossible to miss him!' thought Ronald.   'In another second the scoundrel's brains will be blown out.'

*   *   *   *   *

'Bah!' he suddenly said.   'Why should I kill him?'

And he fired the pistol into the air, and sank down on the grass exhausted. Della Rocca's face changed as if by magic. In a moment he was himself again, receiving the congratulations of his seconds. The doctors meanwhile were busy with Ronald, and their verdict was awaited by Stornello and Martini with terrible anxiety. The old Colonel's cheeks were wet with tears, while Stornello grasped Ronald's hand and bid him be of good cheer. The surgeons cut off a portion of his clothes, and examined the wound. It was a fearfully painful moment, and Ronald nearly fainted. Restoratives were administered, and after five dreadful minutes the elder of the medical men spoke.

' The bullet has entered the fleshy part of the thigh, and of course the sinews are all lacerated and several small veins are cut. But I do not apprehend any danger. It will be a long and painful time for the signor, but with care he will be quite restored. We cannot well extract the bullet here. The operation must be performed at the signore's home at Portino. Meanwhile we have stopped the bleeding.'

Soon the bandages were complete, and the assistant went to arrange one of the carriages for the sufferer. Meanwhile some consultation had taken place between Della Rocca and his seconds. Martini had anxiously waited for the surgeon's verdict, and then reported it to the Marchese, who had returned to the chestnut-tree. After some conversation the two stepped forward, their principal following a few steps behind.

'Signori, we wish to declare, on behalf of the Marchese della Rocca, that Mr. Lascelles has borne himself like a true *galantuomo*, and such is emphatically our opinion. The Marchese will be glad to hear that Mr. Lascelles is satisfied.'

'Ask the Marchese to come nearer,' whispered Ronald from his recumbent position on the grass.

Della Rocca came up to him.

'Marchese,' said Ronald, in a clear voice, 'you have had a narrow escape to-day. Take care not to pollute the ears of honest English girls again. They generally have brothers or friends to protect them, and give people like you a *bastonata*. Addio.'

Then he turned his face away and fainted. But the Marchese had gone quickly, and knew it not. Before the enemy Ronald had borne himself bravely.

CHAPTER X.

WHAT THE STENTS SAID.

'My dear Clara,' said George Stent to his wife one evening when he returned from the City, 'do you think you are strong enough to hear some very strange news?'

'Of course I am, George!' replied his wife, who was lying comfortably on the sofa in what had formerly been Ronald's study. 'What is it?'

'I have received a letter from your father—a very remarkable letter?'

'Is anybody ill? Oh tell me at once, George, and don't keep me in suspense with all this preface and preparation!' exclaimed Clara, the Lascelles' blood asserting itself as she sat up.

'No one is ill—that is, your brother Ronald is not quite well. But there is nothing to be alarmed at Do not excite yourself, Clara. Think how bad it is for you in your present condition.'

'I shall be very bad if you don't tell me, George, instead of making all this fuss. What is the matter?'

'Clara, if you are not quiet, I shall not be able to tell you at all. Nothing is the matter—that is, nothing that need frighten you. It is of course annoying, very annoying. But you are scarcely in a fit condition to hear it.'

His wife jumped up from the sofa.

'Give me the letter and have done with it, or you will drive me out of my senses. I am sure Ronald is very ill, perhaps dead!'

'No, dear, indeed not,' replied Mr. Stent, not yet forced out of his calmness ; 'but he has behaved very badly. He has fought a duel.'

Clara had not yet entirely verified Stent senior's

prophecy. She was still not thoroughly imbued with the views and opinions of the clan. She asked anxiously:

'Was he hurt—seriously hurt? I hope he killed the other man.'

'My dear, you should really think of what you are going to say! I am thankful to be able to inform you that the " other man," as you term him, was unhurt, and that your brother has a slight flesh wound which will confine him to the sofa for a few weeks, but is of no serious importance.'

'Is that really all ?' asked Clara. 'Show me papa's letter.'

'Here it is,' replied her husband, handing it to her. 'You see your father very judiciously wrote to me at the office, for fear of startling you in your present condition.'

'Fudge!' was Clara's brief retort, as she eagerly scanned the letter.

It was not a long one, and stated far less than the reader already knows. Ronald, said Mr. Lascelles, was reported to have quarrelled with an Italian noble-man in the card-room at the Club, and by the custom of the country, the matter had to be settled by a duel. Ronald had been wounded, but was progressing favour-ably. His mother and sister were nursing him, and there was no cause for alarm. With fatherly pride, Mr. Lascelles added that his son was much praised for his generosity in firing into the air when his adversary was disarmed. Then followed a few details of the wound, and the treatment. The Consul wound up by expressing some anxiety lest Ronald should fail to obtain an extension of his leave of absence, and begged Mr. Stent to see the chief of his office on his behalf, and to place the case before him, without of course mentioning the cause of Ronald's illness, and he enclosed a letter to the chief from him-self.

Poor Mr. Lascelles could not have applied to a less sympathetic ambassador.

' What folly !' exclaimed Mr. George Stent.   ' Really, Clara, I am surprised at your father.   I should have thought that at his age he would know better !'

' What has poor papa done ?' asked Clara.

' Done ?   Why he actually seems to encourage Ronald in his dissipated and violent conduct.   A quarrel over cards at some club, in the middle of the night.   A nice thing, truly, for an English gentleman to be involved in.   And he wants *me* to speak for him—to take him under my protection, in fact.   I am to go to Somerset House and intercede for a gambler and a bravo !'

' George, how can you use such dreadful words about poor Ronald !'

' My dear Clara, they are quite justifiable,' answered Mr. Stent, angrier than he had ever been in his life before, and the more disturbed that he was asked to interfere on behalf of his disreputable brother-in-law.

Then he took up the Consul's letter again, and looked through it carefully.

'As your father says, "Ronald is *reported* to have quarrelled with an Italian nobleman in the card-room," very likely they quarrelled about something besides cards,' remarked Mr. Stent with great acuteness. 'People don't go and shoot each other on account of a dispute over cards, even in Italy. *I* never had a quarrel while I was there, though they took me into all their clubs.'

'I dare say not,' replied Clara. 'But then you are older than Ronald, and no doubt wiser.'

'I should hope so,' assented her husband. 'I never was such a fool as Ronald, thank God, and none of *us* were ever silly enough to risk our lives for some trumpery rubbish. Clara dear,' he added, after a pause, 'do you feel well enough to drive round to

John's after dinner? I should like to consult him about this matter.'

Clara was not in the humour to fall in with Stent ways this evening.

'No,' she replied decisively; 'I don't. Go there by yourself.'

'My darling,' replied George, 'I could not think of leaving you alone in your present delicate condition. I will send round to see if they can come here.'

And he rang the bell.

Now Clara knew what 'they' signified. It meant John Stent and his wife, and William Stent and his wife, and perhaps Stent senior. Though she had got used to these people, and had almost become one of them, she did not care to hear her brother's conduct discussed in solemn conclave. Wherefore she said:

'Very well, George. But don't expect me to come down. I am too tired.'

'Eliza shall keep you company, my child,' replied George. 'You are quite right not to exert yourself.' Then he despatched messages and notes to rouse his clansmen.

Clara did not seem particularly pleased at the prospect of Eliza's company. This lady, an unmarried sister of George's, was, like all the other members of her family, very good, very pious, and very regular in her habits. But she was not exactly lively. It was, however, very difficult for Clara to tell her husband that his sister sometimes bored her. Mr. Stent would not have shown anger—he very seldom did—but he would have been very deeply grieved, and Clara knew that if she once uttered such an heresy she would never hear the last of it in the shape of hints from George, and gentle complaints that his wife could not hit it off with his own people, quiet moans over the loss of his sister's companionship, and sincere hopes that poor Eliza's feelings were not much hurt. She

11—2

was afraid of the consequences of speaking, and there-
.ore held her peace.

The moment the dessert was on the table she retired
to her boudoir, and in a very few minutes the clansmen
began to arrive.   With his invariable courtesy, George
went out into the passage to meet his relations, as the
successive carriages stopped at the door.   The greeting was invariably the same :

'What is wrong, George ?   Surely not Clara——'
For the impression had gone abroad that possibly the
expected baby might have come too soon.

George always answered sadly, with a significant
pressure of the hand :

'No, Clara is all right ; but she wants to be quiet
to-night.   Come into the dining-room, and you shall
hear all about it.   Perhaps Jane will be kind enough
to sit in the drawing-room for the present ?'

Soon John, William, Mr. Stent senior, and Mr.
William C. Stent were assembled round the dining-

table, while Jane, Mary, and Susan wondered together, in the first-floor, what it was all about, and 'hoped the gentlemen' would soon come up and tell them.

Downstairs George solemnly pulled out Mr. Lascelles' letter, and handed it first to his father. From Stent senior it passed on to John Stent; then William Stent read it in silence; and finally it reached William C. Stent. Meanwhile George quietly passed the claret and courteously pressed each member of his family to take a glass.

'Now you have all read this extraordinary letter,' said he solemnly, when William C. Stent had folded it up and returned it, 'what course should I pursue under the circumstances? I have asked you here to take your advice on the subject, and shall, as a matter of course, follow that advice.'

'I perceive, George,' said Mr. Stent senior, 'that Mr. Lascelles (who, by-the-by, appears to me to be a rather weak father) does not seem very sure of the cause of this unfortunate quarrel.'

'I noticed that,' came from his sons and his nephew.

'You all know young Ronald Lascelles,' said George; 'he is a wild young fool, capable of any sort of extravagance.'

'A pleasant sort of young man, too,' William C. ventured to observe.

'Very pleasant! oh yes; no one denies that!' chimed in the eldest.

'But rather unreliable, eh?' suggested John.

'Entirely,' assented George.

'Altogether unsteady?' asked the father.

'I should think so,' again said George.

'Quite irregular in his habits?' inquired William.

'Oh, dreadfully!' assented Ronald's brother-in-law. 'He was here for more than a year, and I know all about him.'

'It was very good of you to have him,' observed Mr. Stent senior.

'Very,' chorused the others.

'Then he is not likely to get on?' asked William C.

No answer was vouchsafed to so idle a question. A smile of contempt only played on the lips of the clansmen.

'Does he pay his bills?' asked Stent father.

'No—at least, not all of them. Some come for him here now,' replied George.

'I feared as much,' muttered the old gentleman, with a groan. 'He is a bad lot.'

There was a responsive sigh from the whole company.

George, however, wanted some more positive instructions.

'What am I to do?' he asked. 'If I refuse, I should quarrel with my father-in-law.'

'Never have a quarrel in the family,' observed John sententiously.

'Exactly so,' said George; 'I want to avoid one.'

Then they consulted and discussed. Could George conscientiously interfere on behalf of a young man so utterly lost to every sense of propriety? John and William held that he could not. Mr. Stent senior and William C. were inclined to think that, notwithstanding Ronald's undoubted wickedness, regard for the credit of a connection ('only a *connection*, mind,' observed the old gentleman) was a sufficient reason for assisting him in the way suggested. Perhaps there was in the mind of the younger man some faint recollection of youthful escapades which had remained unknown and undiscovered, but of which the consciousness inclined him to leniency, while Mr. Stent senior thought of a disreputable old uncle, the only black sheep in the clan for three generations, who was pensioned off in a distant French town on condition of never troubling them more.

Unanimity was always the aim of the Stent family; wherefore, after spending an hour over the dining-table without arriving at it, they adjourned to the drawing-room to discuss the matter afresh with the assistance of Mary, Susan, and Jane. Eliza, being unmarried, was not summoned to the council, 'for,' whispered George, 'there might be a woman in the case, you know, and girls ought not to know anything about that sort of thing.'

The fair sex always inclines to gentle measures when the culprit is young and good-looking. Ronald had been polite and nice even to such tremendous bores as Susan and Mary. Jane was more than he could stand, and she had been mortally offended at his refusing to join the fortnightly family dinner at her house, after having borne it six times. So Jane joined her husband William and her brother-in-law John in recommending a courteous but decided refusal, which would of course be followed by the formal and official exclusion of Ronald from the Stent family. He should be to them as if he had never existed. Young men who got into debt and fought duels were not fit company for pious and reputable English households. But Jane and her allies were in the minority. George inclined to the opposition in order not to grieve his wife, so it was finally decided by five votes to three that George should write to Mr. Lascelles, expressing regret at his son's wound, and promising to see the chief of the office at Somerset House immediately.

But it was understood that the ambassador was not justified in telling any falsehoods, and must, therefore, if pressed to do so, state the cause of Ronald's illness.

CHAPTER XI.

OF course in a place like Portino the duel could not remain long a secret. On the morning after it had taken place the police were instructed to prevent it, and the outskirts were carefully patrolled all day. Only in the afternoon did the Prefect hear that it was all over, and that as nobody was killed, and nobody feared another breach of the peace, there was nothing now to do.

This active and zealous officer, who had been appointed to his post for the same reasons that most other officials in Italy obtain theirs, namely, that he had a 'good friend' in power somewhere, was much grieved at the news having reached him so late, and would probably even now have arrested the only man he could get hold of—Della Rocca having at once left by steamer—if he had not discovered that Ronald was under the roof of the British Consul. So the flag saved the wounded hero from a certain amount of worry.

When Mrs. Lascelles had overcome the first shock of alarm, she arranged matters as sensibly and as calmly as any woman could. What was to be feared was fever, for the patient was nervous and excitable. They therefore engaged a nurse to assist in watching him at night, while Teresina, Mrs. Lascelles herself, and old Lina would do the rest.

Quiet was the chief medicine required to restore Ronald to health and strength. The doctors prohibited his talking more than was absolutely necessary, and no one was allowed to worry him with questions. But Count Stornello and Colonel Martini, who called daily to inquire, were severely cross-examined by the anxious parents. They had to give a full account of the duel, which of course they did most willingly, not forgetting to dwell on Ronald's pluck in bearing fearful pain like a Spartan. But they were also repeatedly pressed as to the cause of the duel. As long as the two were at the Consulate together, they stuck manfully to the story about a quarrel over cards; but when the next day Stornello called alone to see his friend, Mrs. Lascelles was waiting for him in the antechamber. She made him come into her drawing-room, and there coaxed, flattered, soothed, and exercised all those wiles which only women can practise, in order to find out the real reason of the duel.

Rumours of a slight disturbance at the Palazzo Donati had that morning reached her ears; and she had therefore something to go upon. Poor Stornello grew terribly uncomfortable under her scrutinizing glance, his natural truthfulness having to be set aside by his sense of loyalty. Bit by bit she wormed the truth out of him, and he left the Consulate in a very depressed frame of mind, to go and confess to the Colonel that he had betrayed all.

When Stornello had sadly and humbly taken his leave, Mrs. Lascelles rejoiced greatly. She had known better than her son himself how much he loved that girl! Could there be a doubt about it now? Of course not! Men did not risk their lives for young ladies who were indifferent to them. Out of evil good would come. If, as she fully believed, her son soon regained his health and strength, she would consider this duel the most fortunate event that could have happened. For of course now, not only must Edith be madly in love with him, but Mr. Woodall could not decently refuse to do all in his power for his daughter's brave champion. And a flush of real pride rose to her face as she thought of her son's courage and noble forbearance. In these reflections she was disturbed

by Mr. Lascelles, who came up from his office to inquire how his son was getting on. When she had
satisfied him on this score she said :

'This is a most fortunate occurrence, Robert, if we
look at it in its proper light !'

'How so, my dear ? I should have thought it was
most *un*fortunate ! Ronald's leave expires next week;
he was to leave us on Monday. Dr. Salviati says he
cannot be moved from his bed for at least a fortnight,
and will not be able to travel for weeks. I must say
I think it deuced unlucky ! Of course, the boy may
not have been able to help it, but he was certainly prejudiced against that Della Rocca to begin
with !'

'My dear Robert,' answered his wife, when she
obtained a chance of putting a word in, 'I am thinking of much more important matters than Ronald's
leave of absence.'

'I do not see how anything can be more important

just now. They gave him three months, which is a very great deal for a junior clerk, and I don't think they will extend it; certainly not if the cause of his illness is known. I have just written to Stent to ask him to see Mr. Charteris, the chief of the office at Somerset House.'

'Never mind Somerset House, Robert. Our boy can do better than earn a hundred and twenty a year as junior clerk.'

'I wish I saw my way to something better for him!' said Mr. Lascelles, with a sigh.

'You dear blind old Robert! Don't you see that he is over head and ears in love with Edith Woodall, and that he fought this duel because he was jealous of that Italian's attentions to her?'

'Whew!' whistled the Consul. 'How do you know all that?'

'I have made Count Stornello confess all about it. He knew a good deal, and anyone can guess the rest,' replied Mrs. Lascelles. 'Stornello admits that the quarrel at the Club was all nonsense—a got-up thing, in fact, to prevent Edith being talked about by all the young men in Portino.'

'Well, I must confess that I was much surprised to hear of Ronald quarrelling over cards,' said the Consul. 'I have never known him gamble, and I should have heard of it soon enough if he had done so at the Club. In fact, I was much more vexed about that than about the duel.'

'Don't worry any more about it, Robert. He does not gamble. I don't believe he touches a card once a month. I understood just now from Stornello that he was jealous of the Marchese's great attention to Edith Woodall, and interfered somehow to prevent it. I could not make out exactly what he did, and I don't think the Count himself quite knew. But at any rate Signor della Rocca insulted Ronald, and he had to fight.'

VOL. I.   12

'That is a very different story!' remarked Mr. Lascelles. 'Now I begin to understand!'

'It is about time you did!' exclaimed his wife. 'Fancy accusing our poor boy of gambling!'

'But,' urged the Consul, 'I don't see how that mends matters. It is only another trouble for the lad. His heart is touched, poor fellow, as well as his leg, that is all. And I fancy the leg will be cured soonest.'

'*I* don't agree with you,' said his wife, smiling.

'Why not? What is your opinion, dear?'

'Why, you old goose!' she exclaimed, 'you stick in the office all day, and never see anything, and when you do creep out of your hole you sit down to your stupid rubber, and know nothing of what goes on; otherwise you could not have helped noticing.'

'Noticing what?' asked Mr. Lascelles.

'Why, that Edith Woodall is quite as fond of the boy as he is of her! I know her well—we have both known her ever since she was a baby. She is not a bit of a flirt, but as good and sensible a creature as ever lived——'

' Well ?'

' Well, if it had been any other girl I should have declared that she flirted outrageously with Ronald.'.

' Oh ! just at one dance !' observed Mr. Lascelles.

' No, not at this one dance only. Ever since Ronald has been here this time they have been constantly together, and the girl is evidently as pleased with his company as he is with hers. Trust a mother's eyes, Robert ! They always see better than a man's in such matters !'

' Very possibly you are right, dear. But supposing it were so, I don't think Woodall would let his girl marry Ronald.'

' I do, then,' replied Mrs. Lascelles. ' In fact I am sure he would have consented, even without this duel. But don't you see how this helps the matter on ? Why, without any of our doing, all Portino will be

12—2

talking about it to-morrow, and Ronald will be the hero of the day. He was wounded in defence of Edith! Think what an effect that must have. Why, Woodall would be a brute if he refused his consent under such circumstances, and then, of course, Ronald's fortune is made.'

'Woodall has certainly always told me,' said the Consul reflectively, 'that he intended to go back to England as soon as he could get a suitable man to take his place here, and that if his daughter's choice fell on such a man, he would be very pleased.'

'Well, and can he have a better one than Ronald?' asked his mother. 'Everybody likes him; he knows Portino as well as Woodall himself, and he speaks Italian like a native.'

'But he has not got sixpence,' objected Mr. Lascelles.

'The Woodalls have enough for all,' retorted his

wife. 'It seems to me as clear as noonday. Nothing could be more suitable, and we should have Ronald and his wife settled happily here close to us.'

'Are you *quite* sure, dear, that the young people are fond of each other ?' asked the Consul again, still believing that his wife's statement of the case was too good to be true.

'I have been quite certain about Edith for some time, and now I am quite sure of Ronald as well,' replied Mrs. Lascelles. 'He has had some foolish misgivings about not loving her enough to marry her——'

'Then you have spoken to him on the subject ?'

'Oh yes ! before the duel. The poor boy is not allowed to talk now. He was afraid he did not love her as much as she deserved, and all that sort of thing. Every word proved to me that he was extremely fond of her, and now, of course, I can have no doubt whatever.'

'Well, dear, possibly you are right. Indeed, now you have shown me the matter in a new light, I hope you are,' said the Consul. 'Shall I say anything at present?'

'Not a word, you old goose,' answered Mrs. Lascelles, kissing him; 'you would only spoil everything. Just hold your tongue, and don't interfere. Men always make a mess of these things.'

Mr. Lascelles nodded good-humouredly.

'All right,' he said.

And thus another mesh was added to the net which was soon to hem Ronald in on all sides.

His mother's prophecy was a true one. Next day Ronald was the hero of the English colony and of Portino. The Italian doctors, accustomed to the dash of their fellow-countrymen which is at once destroyed by the sight of blood, talked everywhere of the extraordinary fortitude of the young Englishman, who, though grievously wounded, had refused to give in, and had steadily walked ten paces towards his adversary. Stornello and Martini, though they endeavoured to conceal the real cause of the duel, made no secret of their principal's conduct, and praised his pluck and generosity to the skies. Smarting under a most painful wound, and having the adversary who had inflicted it entirely at his mercy, he had declined to take any advantage of his position, and had given his life back to the trembling Della Rocca. The latter's fears had not escaped his seconds, who were scarcely less warm in their admiration for Ronald than his own friends. So, of course, the news soon reached Mr. Woodall's bank.

It was first told to one of the clerks over the counter, but scarcely believed. Then another customer confirmed it; then, as it happened, Stornello came in with a cheque, and the cashier took the liberty to ask him about the matter. All the clerks gathered round to listen, and other customers had to wait, which, being Italians and therefore fond of gossip, they did not mind at all.

The head clerk invented some excuse to go into Mr. Woodall's room, and there imparted the astounding information to his principal. The latter at once came out from his sanctum and dragged Stornello in, to hear the tale from his own lips. But the young Count, fresh from his interview with Mrs. Lascelles, was determined to be very careful this time, and mentioned a quarrel at cards as the cause of the duel.

'Oh, dear!' said Mr. Woodall quite sadly; 'I am sorry to hear that the young man gambles.'

'He never gambles, signore!' exclaimed Stornello hotly.

'But you say this was a quarrel over cards,' remarked the banker, rather surprised at Stornello's vehemence.

Quite a chance, signore—an unfortunate chance.

Rinaldo religiously abstains from cards at the Casino. I have never seen him play there before !'

'Oh !' said Mr. Woodall, a little puzzled.

But, of course, being far less interested than Mr. Lascelles, he did not cross-examine his informant. All he did was to send a friendly note of inquiry to the Consulate, hoping that Ronald's wound was progressing favourably. And he went home to dinner a little sooner than usual. Edith, as was her wont, met him in the corridor when she heard his step. When he told her what had occurred, she suddenly turned pale and seized a table with her hand. Mr. Woodall was quite frightened.

'What is it, darling ?' he exclaimed. 'I had no idea it would alarm you so. Young Lascelles is, I understand, getting on very well indeed. You need not be so put out.'

'Tell me all about it, father,' she said. 'It was foolish of me, but the news rather upset me. I thought of poor Mrs. Lascelles.'

This was probably the first story the girl had ever told, and as she told it the blood, which had deserted her face, came rushing back till her very forehead and neck were suffused with blushes. Mr. Woodall led her back into the room, and noticed that she was still trembling.

'My poor child!' he said, 'don't be frightened; there is really nothing to distress you.'

But there was more than Mr. Woodall supposed. At every moment she expected him to say that Ronald had fought for her sake. For Edith, with the quick instinct of budding love, had at once guessed why Ronald had fought this duel. He had exposed his life for her, to shield her from the insolence of the Marchese! He need not have done it, she thought; the Marchese was hardly even disagreeable, and there was no cause to take serious steps. But how noble of him! Only when her father told the whole story, she became quieter. For Ronald had been so thoughtful as to keep her out of it altogether, so that no one but herself could possibly guess the real reason of the encounter. How truly generous and brave! When Mr. Woodall remarked that the lad appeared to have been hasty, and had no business to have quarrelled over cards, her blue eyes sparkled, and she exclaimed, 'Oh, I am sure he never played cards, papa!' which made Mr. Woodall ask sharply 'What *she* knew about it?' So that she blushed again, and stammered very foolishly. But then the banker went on to say that young Lascelles seemed to have behaved very pluckily, and also quite handsomely, and poor Edith blushed again, though this time with pleasure. She could not help murmuring, 'He is very good,' which Mr. Woodall considered rather a singular comment on the affair. And when he had done his story, she asked him so many questions about it that he could not reply to them, and advised her to go and see Mrs. Lascelles after dinner. As this was exactly what

Edith herself wished, she agreed without much demur.

Ronald's friends at Portino evidently did *not* take the same view of the duel as his connections in London.

CHAPTER XII.

THE MAIDEN'S SECRET.

EDITH was shown into the empty drawing-room. 'The signorina is not very well,' said Luisa, as she departed to announce the visitor to Mrs. Lascelles.

Soon Teresina opened the door, and the girls flew into each other's arms.

'How is he?' asked Edith. 'What a dreadful thing!'

'Oh, dear!' replied Teresina, bursting into tears. 'He is not nearly so well to-night. They have to put ice on his head and on his poor leg.'

Edith felt herself turning very pale.

'What is the matter?' she asked.

'Fever, they say,' answered Teresina, between her sobs. 'Oh, Edith dear, if you knew how good he was! Darling Ronald!'

'I know he was very kind and nice,' said Edith, who would have liked to cry also, and thought that her words sounded very cold and unsympathetic.

'You *can't* know! How should you?' cried the young girl almost angrily. 'You are not his sister. But you are fond of him, are you not?' she asked innocently.

Edith turned scarlet again, and looked into the tear-stained face of her friend scrutinizingly. The troubled but transparent gaze reassured her. Teresina, at any rate, had not guessed her secret.

'Of course I like him very much!' she answered, kissing the girl, 'as I like you all—particularly you, dearest.'

Things were progressing rapidly; for this was the second story Edith had told in one evening. Teresina returned her friend's kiss unsuspiciously and went on:

'Fancy, dear; he actually took me and young Signor Donati out for a sail in the yacht! Oh, I was so horribly wicked!'

'Wicked, my darling!' exclaimed Edith; 'why what on earth do you mean?'

'How could I guess that dear, brave Ronald had to fight a duel? And his nasty, cross, selfish sister actually worried him to stop out longer, and chattered to him all the time. How mad he must have felt!'

'When did he take you out?' asked Edith eagerly, scarcely understanding Teresina's self-reproaches.

'Why, yesterday—the very day of the duel!' replied the young girl. 'Only think! He knew he was going to fight that horrid Marchese, and instead of spending his time with his friends, he actually devoted it all to poor naughty me!'

'How nice of him!'

'Nice! You call everything nice, Edith. It may be a proper word, but *I* think it very cold. It was heroic! Why, a few hours later he had to fight for his life! And I made him wretched by worrying! And do you know, Edith,' here she lowered her voice to a whisper, 'I almost cried because he was so determined to go home, and thought it so unkind of him.'

'But, my poor pet, you knew nothing at all about it!' said Edith consolingly.

'Of course I did not! I should have told papa directly, and he would have stopped it,' exclaimed Teresina. 'Oh dear! it is all my fault,' she went on; 'if I had been a clever, sensible girl I should have seen that poor Ronald had something on his mind, and I should have got it all out of him!' Then the sobs began afresh.

Edith was burning to ask for details as to the sufferer's condition, and the prospects of its improving. But poor Teresina was not able to give them. Fresh tears and cries of despair were all that Edith could elicit from her. At last Luisa came in, bringing some tea ; and when she saw the pale, anxious faces of the girls, she exercised the authority of an old servant and walked Teresina off, apologizing with native grace for the poor reception Edith had had.

Very sadly did the latter walk home, leaning on Marietta's arm. Then she retired at once to her room. Ronald was very ill. He might die; and if he died, she, Edith Woodall, had caused his death. She tried to think what the future would be without Ronald. She was surprised to find how great a part Ronald played in her own life. He had not been much at Portino until recently, and yet everything she now cared about seemed connected with him somehow. She could not think of even such a trifle as croquet without Ronald. The game she thought herself so fond of (it was then in the height of its popularity) would be rubbish if he were not there.

And how wicked now to let her thoughts dwell on croquet, while Ronald was groaning on a sick-bed, wounded nigh unto death for her sake! She bitterly repented having danced so often with Della Rocca. Of course if she had not given the Marchese any encouragement Ronald would not have quarrelled with him. How dreadful of her! And she had been so flippant when he had spoken to her about the Italian. No wonder the poor fellow was angry.

Suddenly she felt herself blush at a thought that struck her. Was Ronald fond of her? She knew he had fought for her, and for her sake only; so much was certain. But was he very fond of her as well? or did he only fight because he did not like to see an English girl, an old friend, persecuted by disagreeable attentions? In a tumult of emotion at the vista thus opened up, Edith could not for some time collect her faculties to reason the matter out. She was an eminently sensible girl, and she would not be carried away by a silly fancy. She would think it over calmly and logically. Did men generally fight duels for girls they did not care about ? She thought not. At any rate it was not usual. On the other hand, it had been for centuries understood and accepted that lovers should draw the sword in defence of their lady-loves. Certainly, then, it appeared probable that Ronald *did* care a little. A little ! And then it flashed across her that he must have cared enough to risk his life, and that that precious life was still in peril. What mattered it, then, whether he loved her or not if he was going to die ? Die, because she chose to flirt with an Italian Marchese ! How she hated that Italian. She would have strangled him with her own slender fingers if he had been within her reach. And now she could do nothing but wait and pray. She could not even help to nurse Ronald ; it would not be considered proper. Oh ! if she could only just do one little thing for him, if she were only allowed to run

13—2

errands and carry messages, what a relief it would be!
But she must not betray her secret; she must not let
anyone suspect the real cause of the duel! She would
never hold up her head again in Portino if it were
known! For of course they would all blame her, and
justly too, and say that she had gone on dreadfully
with the Marchese, and make matters out even worse
than they were; for Portino was a gossiping place.
They would whisper about her everywhere, and say
that the gallant young man had fought for a very
unworthy object.

She was very miserable during the long hours of
that night. Even if Ronald recovered, she felt that
she would never be her own self again. Probably he
despised her, and had only fought for her as a matter
of duty. He was right to despise her; she knew she
was quite unworthy of him. He had spent several
years in London, and had gone everywhere, and had
seen the most attractive and charming ladies in Eng-

land; and she was quite a plain provincial, getting her fashions at second-hand, and knowing nothing of the great world in which Ronald had moved. Of course he had seen and *could* see nothing in her except an old friend. He was good and kind to her, and had spoken very sweetly at the fatal dance, but then that was Ronald's way! He was such a dear fellow, so bright and pleasant, and always ready to oblige everyone, and anxious to please. And now, of course, whenever he felt a pang from his wound he would think that *she* had caused it, and would not only despise her, but hate her altogether. She would deserve it all. She would look after her father's house, and would leave off going out, and not care about anything, and certainly, oh certainly, never marry. Of course not, that was out of the question.

At last her weary eyes closed, and her hot head found rest on the pillow moist with tears. Mr. Woodall was quite shocked at her appearance

next morning.   Never had his daughter looked so
pale, and Edith required colour to make her attractive.
To-day she had dark rims under her dim eyes, her
cheeks were quite white, and—dreadful though true—
her nose was red.   It has already been mentioned
that Edith's nose was larger than the conventional nose
of a heroine in a novel.   If she has thereby lost the
reader's sympathy it is her misfortune, not the fault of
the accurate story-teller.

'What is the matter, Edith?' asked the banker
anxiously; 'you look quite ill.'

'Nothing particular, papa,' she answered.   'I was
rather upset last night at the Consulate; that is
all.'

'Marietta told me that Ronald Lascelles was
feverish,' said Mr. Woodall, 'but that ought not to
upset you, Edith.'

Put in so simple and plain a form, it certainly
ought *not* to have affected Edith's appearance.   But

her woman's wit was equal to the emergency, and she was able, this time, to confine herself pretty well within the bounds of truth:

'Poor little Teresina was so dreadfully cut up,' she said, 'and did nothing but cry and sob and reproach herself for having gone out sailing with Ronald Lascelles.'

And at the recollection Edith herself could scarcely repress her tears. She choked them down, however, and busied herself with making tea, and generally attending on her father, and then she endeavoured to talk of other matters till Mr. Woodall took up his *Gazetta di Portino*, and began to scan its meagre columns. Then she hid behind the urn, and pretended to eat, but did little else than cut her roll into small pieces, take them up and put them down again. Mr. Woodall occasionally looked up from his paper. Evidently the news did not interest him as much as usual. He watched his daughter closely.

'You are not eating anything, Edith,' he remarked abruptly.

'I am not hungry, papa dear.'

'What *is* the matter with you?' asked the banker almost impatiently.   'I shall send for Salviati.'

'Please not, papa; I assure you it is nothing!'

'But you look like a ghost, and you have not eaten even a scrap of bread and butter.   There is your egg untouched.'

'I can't eat, papa dear.   I shall be better by-and-by.'

'There is nothing like nipping a complaint in the bud, my child,' answered Mr. Woodall.   'I'll send for the doctor, and he'll tell us whether you're going to have anything the matter with you.'

'Really,' pleaded Edith piteously, 'there is nothing wrong.   I have not slept well, and I was dreadfully shocked last night about all this——'

'That's all very well,' interrupted Mr. Woodall;

'but you ought to have got over it by this time. Young men have fought duels before now, and you did not look like death when you heard about it. Now be a good girl, and drink some tea at once.'

Mr. Woodall had spoken throughout in a good-natured tone, and his words sounded far kinder than they may appear in print. But his persistence and his curious glances alarmed Edith. She drank some tea, and tried to take a spoonful of egg.

'That's right, Edith,' said her father encouragingly. 'After all, you know, the young man is no relation, though we have always been great friends with the Lascelles. I should be awfully sorry if anything were to happen to him. Halloo!'

The exclamation was caused by Edith suddenly raising her pocket-handkerchief to her eyes and bursting into tears. In another moment she rushed from the room with an inaudible apology.

Mr. Woodall put down his paper altogether. He

looked after her for a minute or two with a puzzled, solid expression. 'What is all this about?' thought he. 'These are not Edith's ways. She is a sensible girl, and does not indulge in hysterics, nor fainting fits, nor any other female fads. There must be something more behind it.' And Mr. Woodall resolved to watch his daughter closely, and not to speak of the duel for a day or two.

Perhaps old Marietta had a shrewd suspicion of what was going on in her young mistress's heart. At any rate Edith was not disturbed for an hour, after which the old woman appeared with a cup of strong beef-tea. At first Edith declined to take it, but she was soon bribed by the suggestion that perhaps, when the signorina had taken it, she would feel strong enough to walk along the Via Marina and inquire how the signorino cavaliere had passed the night.

It was strange how quickly that beef-tea restored her. In less than ten minutes they were facing a strong sirocco, and trying to keep their umbrellas steady to shelter them from the pelting showers. But, wet and windy as it was, Edith stopped as they crossed the market-place. The stalls were all turned to leeward, and the women who had no stalls had taken refuge under the columned portico of Santissima Annunziata. But there were flowers in abundance, all the more for the warm spring showers. Disdaining the artfully made-up bouquets, Edith bought a great bunch of fragrant white roses, and then walked on silently to the Consulate.

To-day she was not kept waiting long in the empty drawing-room. Mrs. Lascelles came in almost at once. A glance at the mother's face, and the harrowing anxiety disappeared from Edith's heart.

'He is better!' she exclaimed, rushing forward.

'Much better, my dear! He is fast asleep; he has slept ever since two o'clock this morning. We are all so much relieved. Nothing but quiet is now neces-sary.'

Edith looked positively radiant.

'I am so glad!' she said; 'and—papa will be so pleased.'

Then the two sat down and talked—Edith shy and blushing, Mrs. Lascelles demonstrative and affec-tionate—and after a short stay the girl rose, and, pointing to her flowers, said:

'Do you think he could bear the smell?'

'Why not, dear?' asked Mrs. Lascelles. 'He is extremely fond of roses, and I am sure when he wakes he will be glad to see them by his side, and still more pleased when he knows who sent them.'

'But,' stammered Edith, 'don't say they came from me!'

'Very well,' answered Mrs. Lascelles, smiling; 'I will tell him that Mr. Woodall sent them. He will think it very kind of your father.'

The girl blushed again.

'No, no!' she exclaimed, 'he knows that papa would not send him flowers. Just put them in his room and say nothing.'

'Just as you please, dear,' Mrs. Lascelles said good-humouredly. 'And now good-bye; I am going to look after my invalid.'

Edith bad her farewell, and kissed her. To her surprise Mrs. Lascelles put an arm round her neck and whispered:

'I know why they fought, Edith dear. Your secret is safe with me.'

Then she pressed the girl's hands warmly, and swiftly ascended the stairs, leaving her wondering and scarlet.

Thus was another mesh woven of the net which was to enclose Ronald in its trammels.

CHAPTER XIII.

THE MESHES ARE WOVEN.

Mrs. LASCELLES was the very best mother in a world which is, fortunately for male mankind, full of good mothers. She never lost her head for a moment during Ronald's illness. She was ever watchful, but never fussy. Everything was done that could be done, and no precaution was neglected, and yet the patient knew but little of all the trouble taken, and was ignorant of the endless though individually trifling measures adopted in obedience to the instructions of the doctors. He was not only told 'not to worry'—an instruction so easy to give and so difficult for sick men to obey—but every cause of worry was sedulously removed. On the Monday following he should, according to previous arrangement, have started for London, and though of course it was impossible for him even to leave his bed, on which a huge apparatus protected the wounded limb from the slightest touch, he became restless when the day arrived, and there was a return of feverishness.

'Do not be anxious, said Mrs. Lascelles, when she noticed that his thin cheeks were flushed and his eyes brighter than usual. 'Your father has arranged for an extension of leave.'

Mrs. Lascelles was not absolutely correct in her statement. No answer from Mr. Charteris had yet arrived, and the Consul entertained serious doubts as to the reception his request would meet with. But she thought that it was her duty to her son to put matters in the most favourable light possible. Visits of inquiry and condolence had been numerous. Some of the callers had been impelled by motives of curiosity, and all would have been glad to be certain of the real cause of the duel. It had been whispered about in some quarters, and the gossips of Portino even went so far as to say that the Marchese had grossly insulted Miss Woodall in Ralph's hearing. But then the gossips of Portino were not more careful in their statements than those of other towns, wherefore people would have been glad to know the truth from Mrs. Lascelles herself.

That lady thought that she held the trump cards, and was not in a hurry to play them. She evaded most of the questions, and assumed an air of mystery which only stimulated curiosity still further. When Ronald was out of danger, she confided to a few chosen female friends, under the strictest promise of secrecy, that the real cause of the duel was Ronald's jealousy of the Marchese's attentions to Edith Woodall. When her friends asked, as they naturally did, whether the young people were engaged, Mrs. Lascelles at once said :

'No! certainly not! But my boy undoubtedly admires her very much. It is a pity that we are so badly off! I never regretted being poor so much as I do now. He has not proposed to her, because she is so rich. But of course this is quite strictly private.'

'Of course,' the friendly gossip would reply, though already debating whom she should first tell. Then, after some sympathetic words from her friend, Mrs. Woodall would go on:

'You see, he is so proud. Everybody says he be- haved wonderfully on that dreadful day, under the most trying circumstances. But he would not have it said that he married Edith Woodall for her money. It would kill him.'

Thus Mrs. Lascelles' chosen allies went away with the conviction that Ronald was deeply in love with Edith, and that the affection was mutual, but that the young man was too high-minded to take advantage of this circumstance. And as the matter was discussed by at least half a dozen ladies with closed doors, the English colony knew all about it the next day. By noonday Ronald was a greater hero than ever, and while the ladies praised his nobility of character and his good looks, the men called him a real brick, and thought that he was almost too high-minded for a mercenary world. On that morning even Mr. Woodall obtained an inkling of what was going on. A merchant on 'Change asked him very pointedly how Miss Woodall was.

'Very well, thank you,' answered the banker; and as he was still preoccupied about her health, he added quickly, 'Why should she be otherwise?'

'I thought this duel must have affected her much,' replied the speaker, under the impression that Mr. Woodall of course knew all about it.

'Oh! She was upset for the moment, but she is all right now, thank you,' replied he.

'I am glad to hear it. Please present my compliments,' his friend went on innocently, 'it is not every young lady who has so gallant a champion as Mr. Lascelles. Good-day.'

Mr. Woodall stared after the departing merchant. Suddenly he understood why Edith had been so agitated, had lost her appetite, and had burst into tears. Good heavens! The young people were in love with each other, and Ronald Lascelles had fought the Marchese for the sake of his daughter!

Mr. Woodall walked home very thoughtfully. He was serious, very serious, but he did not look cross or angry. On the contrary, he spoke to his clerks in a gentler tone than usual, and was more patient than he generally was with a couple of importunate idlers who gained admittance into his back room.

Mrs. Lascelles' private information to her friends had borne fruit even more quickly than she herself could have hoped. She did not expect that Mr. Woodall would so soon obtain the key to his daughter's pallor and to her frequent visits to Teresina. She had only wished to prepare the ground, and to gain all Portino to her side of the question. She was reinforced in an unexpected manner by two letters which Mr. Lascelles brought up to her in the afternoon.

One was from George Stent. It ran as follows:

' Dear Mr. Lascelles,

'We were much grieved at the intelligence conveyed in your favour of the 8th inst. Both Clara and myself are sincerely sorry to hear that Ronald is hurt, and that his recovery is not likely to be rapid. But our sorrow on this account is far surpassed by the pain we feel at the young man having committed so wrong and unchristian an act as to fight a duel, and for so paltry and wicked a cause as a quarrel over cards. We will not, however, add to the natural grief which you and Mrs. Lascelles must feel, by any condemnatory remarks.

'In compliance with your request, I called this morning on Mr. Charteris, and delivered your letter. He informed me that he would reply to it himself, but I gathered that he was not very favourably disposed towards your unfortunate son. I cannot say that I am surprised at this circumstance.

'Clara continues as well as can be expected. I have dissuaded her from writing herself, as she is naturally much disturbed by her brother's misconduct. It is, indeed, fortunate that the news, owing to the precautions I took, has had no serious consequence. She sends her best love to you, Mrs. Lascelles, and her sister. With kind regards, believe me to remain,

'Dear Mr. Lascelles,

'Yours very sincerely,

'GEORGE STENT.'

'What a heartless, odious letter!' exclaimed Mrs. Lascelles. 'Poor Clara! I had no idea he was such a cold-blooded creature, had you?'

'No, indeed,' exclaimed the Consul, 'or I would never have sanctioned the marriage, notwithstanding all his money. He is a prig! Fancy condoling with us on poor Ronald's misconduct, as he calls it.'

'Yes, and saying that he won't add any condemnatory remarks. It is too bad. Yet, somehow, he does not seem to make Clara miserable. She always writes as if she adored him.'

'Perhaps she does,' said Mr. Lascelles, shrugging his shoulders, a gesture acquired by long residence in Italy; 'tastes differ. But look at this! It makes matters worse.'

'This' was a letter from Mr. Charteris.

'SIR' (it said),

'In reply to your letter, in which you request further leave of absence for your son, Mr. Ronald Lascelles, on account of his serious illness, I beg to inform you that it is not in my power to grant it, as all requests for leave beyond that allowed by the Departmental rules must be referred to the Treasury. In order, however, to save time, I have transmitted your letter, with the medical certificates enclosed in it, to the Junior Lord, whose decision will in due course be communicated to you.

'I am, Sir,

'Your obedient servant,

'F. G. CHARTERIS.'

'This is not very encouraging, is it?' asked the Consul.

'Indeed it is not!' replied his wife. 'It is all George's fault. What a pity you wrote to him!'

'I regret it bitterly,' said Mr. Lascelles. 'I thought no one would work so heartily for poor Ronald as his brother-in-law. It seems that I was quite wrong, and should have done better to send my letter to Mr. Charteris by post.'

'I do not suppose he will get the extension now,' remarked Mrs. Lascelles. 'What will happen if it is refused?'

'He will be struck off the list, that is all,' replied the Consul.

'Do you know that I shall not be so very sorry? When once that wretched office is off his mind, he will mend much more quickly, and I am sure that then we need not wait long before he is engaged to Edith Woodall.'

'You still think he is fond of her?'

'I am more sure of it than ever.' replied Mrs. Lascelles. 'And as to her, she positively worships him. She is always coming to see Teresina now, and talks to the child for hours about nothing but Ronald. She sends flowers for his room every day. I know they come from her, though the sly puss pretends that they don't.'

'Well, you know best,' answered the Consul, again

shrugging his shoulders. 'But I should be very sorry if Ronald lost his appointment.'

'The very best thing that could happen to him,' the lady said very positively.

And thus another mesh was woven in the net.

Mrs. Lascelles had indeed some grounds for saying that she was more certain than before about Ronald's affection. The young man was ill, therefore easily affected. Of course his mother had made no secret of Edith's frequent visits. She was far too clever to rush in and say that the girl was there again—far too acute to volunteer any statements whatever. But when she arranged the flowers, she took care that Ronald should ask her who had sent them; when Teresina returned to the sick-room to take charge of her brother she did not forget to inquire whether anyone had called, and who. She had been almost triumphant when Mr. Woodall himself looked in on the Sunday, to ask about the invalid's progress; but she had understood how to conceal her triumph. At that time, of course, the banker had known nothing except that there had been a quarrel, and his visit had simply been paid out of kindliness to his old friend the Consul. But Mrs. Lascelles produced the card on the Tuesday, quite accidentally, and watched Ronald's face while he looked at it. It did not, however, tell her very much. She learnt more from his glance of satisfaction when the daily bouquet was brought in.

Few men in rude health know what the sight and perfume of a Marshal Niel rose means to an invalid nailed to his couch. Ronald's pleasure was at first a purely sensual one. He always delighted in flowers, and when he could do nothing but lie on his back and listen to Teresina's reading, he almost yearned for them. They brought him the sun and the fresh air and the blue sky, and he inhaled their intoxicating perfume with positive greed. He took a pale saffron-coloured rose and laid it on the coverlet; he raised it to his face and smelt it; he examined it, and admired it, and smelt it again. All this was merely because he liked roses much, and he was weak and ill, and they pleased him and soothed him. But Mrs. Lascelles made up her mind that he was worshipping the giver; and if she had ever had any doubts at all about the intensity of her son's love for Edith, they now disappeared.

And no doubt Ronald did sometimes—very often, in fact—think of the fair girl who filled the sick-room with flowers, and called so often to hear of his progress. However fond a man may be of his young sister, however much he may adore his mother, the hours are apt to pass heavily when he has absolutely no other company but theirs. The doctors had prohibited visits altogether. Only the nurse, Teresina, and Mrs. Lascelles could be trusted to refuse to talk themselves and to reduce the invalid to silence when he had talked enough. Even the Consul was only allowed five minutes morning and evening. So Ronald had plenty of time to think, and he sometimes thought that it would be very pleasant for a change if Edith were there to read to him, or to play to him, or even simply to sit still. He also caught himself wondering what she thought of the duel, and whether she knew why he had fought it. He would have been so glad to see Stornello, or Colonel Martini, or young Donati; for he would have liked to know what Portino said.

A man may be very plucky and single-minded during a duel; but when it is all over, and when he has to bear a long period of confinement, he will not unnaturally begin to think that he ought to get some good by his endurance of suffering. So one day he asked Teresina what was the last news in Portino.

'They say you were brave to fight, and very noble to let the man off,' replied Teresina, kissing him. 'But you must not excite yourself, dear. Dr. Salviati says you must not talk about the duel.'

Further cross-examination was of no use. Teresina knew nothing particular. Gossip had not reached her still juvenile ears. Ronald was determined not to ask his mother, who, as he sometimes expressed it in his own thoughts, 'had gone over to the enemy,' or, in other words, wanted him to marry. He must wait till he was allowed to see his male friends. He had not to wait very long. Before another week was over young Donati, who had often craved admittance, was at last allowed to come in. As he was young and had not been present at the duel, he was considered the most harmless of Ronald's friends. There was of course much hand-pressing and much condolence. Then Ronald looked round, and asked the sick-nurse to fetch him some beef-tea. This he knew would take a few minutes.

'What do they say about the duel, Donati? I mean, about the cause of it?'

'What should they say, *caro mio?* They say you

fought like a lion for the Signorina Woodall, and that she must be very hard-hearted to refuse you !'

'Then they know !' gasped Ronald. 'Who told them ? Who told you ?'

'*Chi lo sa ?* It was in the air ! On Sunday nobody knew. They said you had quarrelled at the Casino. On Tuesday, behold they all knew, even the veriest baby. And they all wish to congratulate ; I first of all, *mio caro amico*——'

The nurse was too quick for the friends. She would not leave her patient long, so simply ordered the beef-tea and returned. The conversation had to be conducted very carefully, and the special subject avoided.

Just when Mrs. Lascelles called Donati away, as his quarter of an hour had expired, the young man stooped over his friend and kissed him in Italian fashion on both cheeks. At the same time he whispered :

'Courage, Rinaldo. The day you can rise, go and ask the *banchiere* for his daughter. Lucky man !'

CHAPTER XIV.

RONALD ASKS QUESTIONS.

MR. CHARTERIS' letter to the Consul was followed, in about a week, by a communication from the Junior Lord of the Treasury. This was couched in warmer and more courteous terms than the Somerset House epistle, for Mr. Lascelles' services were sufficiently well known and appreciated in official circles for him to be treated as a valued public servant.

The letter was marked 'Private and Confidential,' and the writer took the liberty to suggest that the best plan would be for Mr. Ronald Lascelles to send in his resignation on the score of ill-health. 'My Lords,' said the friendly Junior Lord, would scarcely be in a position to grant Mr. Lascelles a further extension of leave. Mr. Charteris had been informed of the applicant's illness and its cause, which would militate seriously against the indulgence requested. It would probably be better for Mr. Ronald Lascelles to resign now, and to make an application for re-admission to the Civil Service at some future time, when he was quite restored to health and the boyish quarrel was forgotten.

Of course Mr. Lascelles attributed this advice entirely to his son-in-law's hostile officiousness. His irritation was extreme, and he vented his anger by a very stiff note to Mr. George Stent, which scarcely ruffled that gentleman at all, as he felt conscious of having done his duty. There was a consultation between the parents and the doctors as to whether Ronald should be informed of the state of things. The matter was urgent; and as the fever had now entirely disappeared, it was determined that the young man should be informed of his altered prospects.

Mrs. Lascelles undertook the task, which was an easy one to her, for reasons already explained.

'George Stent has been very stupid,' she said to Ronald; 'but I think his stupidity will turn out for the best.'

And then she told him what had happened, concluding with the words :

'So now you must not worry about Somerset House. Get well as soon as you can, and then we will talk about what you shall do next.'

'I do not see what I am to do!' said Ronald despondingly.

'Nonsense, Ronald! Why surely you have it all your own way!'

He suspected his mother's drift, but did not, at first, choose to understand.

'Nothing but my father's allowance, and no prospects of a berth !   I do not call that having it all my own way.'

'And a charming girl, with a large fortune, ready to marry you the moment you ask her,' replied his mother, smiling. 'Certainly the prospect is very bad indeed !—but it is one which most young men would envy.'

'I cannot make up my mind about that yet,' answered Ronald.

'Really, you surprise me, dear,' said his mother gently. 'You go and fight a duel because some man pays her attention' (Ronald started), 'you create a sensation in the place; you *pose* as her champion, and get severely hurt on her behalf, and then you say you can't make up your mind. What is it, dear boy, that worries you ?' she asked, gently stroking his soft hair. 'Tell me. No one can be so anxious for your future happiness as I am, and you should confide in me.'

'There is really nothing more to tell, mother, than

what I have already said,' he replied. 'I do not think I love Edith well enough to marry her.'

Mrs. Lascelles smiled, thinking of the duel, and remembering the Marshal Niel roses.

'You need not be afraid, Ronald. There are few men who would coolly expose their lives for a girl, even if they loved her very much. Do you think George Stent would have fought a duel for Clara ?'

'No,' laughed Ronald ; 'it's not in his line.'

'Yet he loves her deeply, I believe, and I think they are very happy. Don't be such a goose, Ronald. I can't understand your doubts. It seems to me that if ever there was a case of love on both sides, this is one.'

'I cannot explain myself, mother, but I suppose you are right after all.'

'Of course I am, Ronald. You may trust my experience.'

The young man did not look quite convinced, but

there was a flush on his cheek which warned his mother that the exciting discussion must not be pursued further. She turned the conversation. Ronald became very silent, and scarcely paid attention to his mother's remarks.

'Do you not think that I might see Stornello, mother?' he asked at length. 'The poor fellow has been here so often, and has never once been admitted; and really I am fit to talk to anyone now.'

Mrs. Lascelles raised no objection, and with a gratified sigh Ronald laid his head back on the pillow. For he had resolved to have a serious talk with his old friend before finally deciding on the step his mother advised so warmly. Stornello was young, he was enthusiastic, he had been—perhaps still was— really in love, and would therefore understand Ronald better than even his mother.

'My dearest friend, how pale you look! *Bontà divina*, what a change!' Such was Stornello's greeting, scarcely quite a judicious one. 'Days I have been waiting to see you, but that *duenna* of yours'—with a glance round to see that they were alone—'is worse than a Cerberus. If I ever have a pretty wife I will appoint that nurse to be house-keeper.'

'The doctors ordered me to keep quiet,' said Ronald.

'Ah, yes! I know, *poverino*. When they once obtain footing in a house, they are like blackbeetles—very difficult to get rid of. But now, I hope, they have done their worst, and soon you will be on your legs again! How pleased we shall be!'

'I shall have to remain on the sofa at least three weeks more, they say,' sighed poor Ronald.

'Three weeks? Impossible! But what of that? Three weeks are nothing, if you can have friends to talk to you, and cheer you, and tell you what they are saying in Portino.'

'What *are* they saying in Portino? That is just what I want to know, Marco,' said Ronald.

'That you are a hero, that Della Rocca is a coward, and that the signorina is a very happy woman. That is what they say, *carissimo*, and they are right.'

'How did they find out that it concerned Miss Woodall?' asked Ronald.

Stornello blushed violently, remembering his cross-examination at Mrs. Lascelles' hands.

'A little bird!' he answered, shrugging his shoulders. 'What would you? These things are found out somehow, however discreet one may be. Remember, there were many present under the portico of the Palazzo Donati.'

'So there were,' assented Ronald.

'And,' Stornello proceeded, gaining courage as he saw that his friend did not suspect him, 'they will talk, you know. There were comparative strangers amongst them—people who had no special reason for silence.'

'It is very annoying!' exclaimed Ronald.

'Annoying! How?' asked the Italian. Why it is a blessing from heaven, since, *caro mio*, you are not killed, for which all the saints be thanked.'

'I do not think it is a blessing that a young lady should be talked about by all the fools in Portino,' growled the invalid.

'Why not, as you are going to marry her? It is quite dramatic! Of course you would not wish the signorina to be talked about in connection with any-one else! But with *you* it is different, being about to become her husband.'

'But I am not, Marco. It is a mistake!'

'How, a mistake?' exclaimed Stornello, quite surprised. 'Surely she is pleased and accepts such a husband as you with delight?—or is it the *vecchio* who objects?'

'No,' answered Ronald quietly; 'it is my own fault. I have not asked her.'

'Oh! on account of your dreadful wound. *Povero*, of course you could not ask her formally. But it is understood. The Signore papa has arranged matters, no doubt?'

'Nothing is arranged. I cannot make up my mind. Listen, Stornello; I want your advice!'

'With the greatest pleasure, Rinaldo. Ha! I comprehend. There is some little affair to settle first; some pretty *contadina*, perhaps? Oh, Rinaldo, I thought you were a serious man. Fie! But command me—I am at your service. And I flatter myself that I can conduct such a negotiation delicately, diplomatically. Do you want money? I have plenty just now; the rents have come in.'

'Do stop, old man! don't hurry on so,' said Ronald, interrupting the Italian's voluble flow of words. 'I thank you from my heart, for I know you have no

more money than you want, and your offers of help
are more valuable even than money.'

'Pooh!' again interrupted Stornello, '*fra amici*——'

'But there is nothing of the sort. What I meant to
ask you is simply whether you think I am in love with
Miss Woodall?'

The Italian stared at him in astonishment. Ronald
repeated the question.

'In love!' gasped he at last. 'Why *certo, certissimo!*
How could it be otherwise? Is she not most graceful
and charming? Rinaldo mio, your wound must have
affected you. You have fever.'

'Not at all,' said Ronald. 'What I cannot decide
is whether I love her enough to marry her!'

This was too much for Stornello. He burst into a
roar of laughter.

'Capital!' he cried. 'Excellent! Here is a young
man who is generally rather cool and *flegmatico*, but
catches fire because a handsome Marchese dances

twice, thrice, with Signorina Edith. He knows her well himself; he dances with her many times. He eclipses the Marchese, and then fights him. And he asks me whether he loves her enough to marry her? Why, *caro mio*, you are not in love like *noi altri*. We first singe our hair a little ; our hearts are perhaps touched. But you burn! The flames consume you ; and as to your heart, why,' and here Stornello placed his hand on his waistcoat, 'it is all gone—all at the Palazzo Woodall !'

'You really think so ?' asked Ronald doubtfully. 'Your judgment is not formed merely by the circumstances of that night ?'

'No !' exclaimed Stornello. 'I have seen it coming ; we have all seen it coming ever since you last returned from England. A blind man could see it. Both of the signori papas must have seen it, and they wagged their old heads and smiled approvingly. Look at the *banchiere* now !'

And Stornello, who was like most Italians a born mimic, cleverly 'made up' his face to resemble Mr. Woodall removing his spectacles and smiling blandly.

There was a knock at the door, and Mrs. Lascelles came in.

'Forgive me, Count Stornello,' she said, 'for interrupting you.'

The young man greeted her courteously and almost affectionately, for he was very fond of the good matron, and she had taken him into her heart when she noticed the frequency of his visits and his anxious inquiries about Ronald. But her liking for him did not prevent her doing her duty.

'You have been half an hour talking, and Ronald is not allowed to excite himself for fear of a return of the fever. I must turn you out, but,' she added, with a smile, 'you may come to-morrow, if you like. He will be glad to see you.'

'Indeed I shall,' said the invalid.

And Stornello, kissing him on both cheeks, bid them good-bye.

The visit was disturbing in its effects. Ronald could think only of the subject discussed, and these thoughts did not conduce to rest. Everybody thought he was in love with Edith, and his best friends laughed at the notion that he did not care for her enough to marry her. They must be right after all. The friendship, the true affection, he felt for the girl *must* be love. It was not quite what he expected love to be, but evidently he had been mistaken. It could be nothing else. Stornello had no interest in the matter except Ronald's own; Stornello had been with him constantly during the past months. He had been perfectly open and frank with the young Italian, who, as an outsider, would see most of the game. Stornello was sure that there was love—not ordinary love, but a violent passion.

Donati too—though Donati, being a mere boy, could

not be expected to know much—expressed the same opinion. And his wise mother entertained no doubts whatever. Certainly then it must be true, and his misgivings were exaggerated and absurd.

She was really a most delightful girl, and he could find no fault with her, except that there floated before him a vision of deep-black eyes, a short nose, and a small mouth with full red lips, which were not Edith's. Did real lovers ever consider their mistress's nose and eyes and lips anything but perfection? Edith's nose was too long, undoubtedly, and her cheek-bones projected too much. Surely that was not a lover's standpoint! If he really loved her, could he criticise her nose and her cheek-bones?

Well, there were certainly many men in love with much uglier women, who had much longer noses and higher cheek-bones. Did these men, he wondered, ever notice their wives' faults? Surely they must. They could not be quite blind. If they looked at a statue, they must perceive that the faces of their lady-loves did not come up to the ideal. That was no reason for not loving a woman! If only ideally beautiful women obtained husbands, what a sad thing it would be for the human race! It must be all nonsense; and how could he expect to find a classical beauty? And over this nonsense, a companion of sense, he at last fell asleep. And he was visited by a dream of a beautiful creature, of imposing figure and rich colour, who seemed instinct with Italian warmth and sunshine. She stretched out a jewelled hand to him, and he clasped it, and awoke. But nevertheless Stornello had woven another mesh in the net—very nearly the last.

CHAPTER XV.

THE CONSUL'S OPINION.

MR. LASCELLES had always been a good father to his children, and they loved him dearly. They could scarcely remember a harsh word from him; and even in Ronald's boyish days, when he had played some tricks which deserved a birching, Mr. Lascelles had only reproached gently. Thus, his children loved him more than they feared him, and it was not surprising that the stronger will of his wife reduced him to a secondary position at home. He was perfectly satisfied with it. She had governed the household with a firm and judicious rule from the first day that she took charge of the then tiny establishment. She had made small means go far even for Italy, and had brought up their children admirably.

During the disturbed political and social times of our story Mr. Lascelles had, of course, been much absorbed by his duties, and by the responsibilities he was obliged to assume. Once he had been for several months the only representative of England in that portion of Italy, for there was no Government to which an envoy could be accredited, and the other towns only possessed native Vice-consuls. So it happened that at the critical period of his two elder children's lives their father was too busy to be consulted by them, too much absorbed to give advice, often even too anxious to listen to them. Hence both Clara and Ronald had come to regard their mother as the ruler and chief of the family. Even when things had to be done which only a father could do, Mrs. Lascelles undertook them. She placed papers to sign before her husband, drafted letters for him, and carried out everything except the more formal work. It was she to whom George Stent had explained his intentions as to Clara's marriage settlement, and it was she who had instructed the lawyers, always, however, careful to keep up her husband's prestige by such phrases as: 'Mr. Lascelles wishes me to tell you,' or 'I will ask Mr. Lascelles what he thinks.'

To talk matters over with his father was therefore an unusual idea for Ronald. Hitherto he had never talked matters over with his father. He had discussed them with his mother, and when a decision requiring Mr. Lascelles's co-operation was arrived at, it was carried out as a matter of course without more ado. But when he woke on the morning after Stornello's visit, and lay on his bed waiting for the nurse to dress his wound, which was still occasionally painful, he decided to have a talk with Mr. Lascelles. There was a faint idea lingering in his breast that his father might not share the general opinion, and would take up the view that he ought not, under the circumstances, to propose to Edith. Every one to whom he had yet spoken seemed to consider him as necessarily engaged to her, or about to be ; and to everyone it appeared so proper, so natural, in fact so inevitable, that, as has already been seen, Ronald had very nearly overcome his scruples and adopted the same opinion. But there was still a chance that his father might disapprove, and, if so, he would, as a dutiful son, follow his father's advice. So when Mr. Lascelles came to inquire after him as usual, he asked whether the Consul could spare a quarter of an hour from the office, and begged Teresina to leave them alone together, which she did with a slight pout on her pretty lips.

'Now that I must resign Somerset House, father, thanks to George's clumsiness, do you see anything for me to do ?'

'Get well as fast as you can, my boy,' answered Mr. Lascelles.

' But afterwards ?'

' Don't worry about afterwards. You must get strong before we need think about anything else.'

' I am improving so much, father, that I shall be about in a very few weeks. It is high time to think of what I am to try next; it is no use my hanging about here, you know.'

' You might help me in the Consulate,' said Mr. Lascelles, ' and of course they would appoint you unpaid vice-consul directly. Then, when I retire you would probably get the place.'

Ronald made a grimace. The prospect of being unpaid vice-consul at Portino for eight or ten years was not particularly attractive, and his father, as he knew, could not afford to retire in less time.

' I am afraid that is not a very bright look-out, father,' he said, ' because I should be many years without earning anything, and you know you cannot afford to keep me.'

'Oh, we could manage well enough if you lived at home,' said Mr. Lascelles.

The Consul evidently did not wish to broach the subject of his son's love affairs. His wife had warned him 'that he would spoil all.' So Ronald had to start upon it himself.

'Do you think I ought to propose to Edith Woodall, father?' he asked abruptly.

Mr. Lascelles looked surprised.

'Ought? what do you mean, my boy? I thought you wished to do so. I understood you were fond of her.'

'Never mind that for the present, father. Do you think there is any necessity for my proposing to her on account of this stupid duel, you know, and all the talk in the place?'

'I think she would be much disappointed if you did not speak,' answered Mr. Lascelles, smiling.

'But not otherwise compromised?' inquired Ronald.

'No, certainly not,' replied the Consul. 'She has behaved very well, and there is nothing to compromise her at present except a little idle gossip, which would soon wear off. But why do you ask such questions, Ronald? Surely you are not afraid of being rejected?'

'No, father; but I am puzzled about two questions. The first is, whether I love her sufficiently to make her as good a husband as she deserves——'

'That you are the only person to judge of,' interrupted Mr. Lascelles. '*I* can't tell you. I should have thought it very easy to make up your mind about it.'

'It is not so easy as you think, father.'

'Well, I never had any doubts about your mother, Ronald. I was afraid she would not have me, but I never feared that I should not be a good husband to her! What a fanciful idea! If you like the girl, and if she loves you, which your mother tells me is the case, why of course you will make her the best husband she can have! Surely that is a matter for *her* to have doubts about, not you! What a queer lot you young fellows are, with your hesitations and uncertainties!'

'Perhaps we are,' said Ronald.

'Why, in my young days, if a fellow liked a girl, he asked her to marry him, and never bothered his head as to whether he was sufficiently in love with her to make her a good husband; and I don't think marriages turned out worse than they do now.'

'Well, father, let us put that aside for a moment. I like Miss Woodall very much——'

'You could not have chosen better, my boy,' interrupted Mr. Lascelles. 'I have known her ever since she was in long clothes, and I have known her father almost since we were boys together.'

That brings me to the second question,' said Ronald. 'Is it fair, do you think, for me to propose

to a girl in such a good position, and considering that
I have nothing at all ?'

'Well, of course she is well off,' replied Mr. Lascelles.
'She has some money of her own from her mother. I
was one of the executors, so I know all about that.
And Woodall is sure to do something handsome for
her. There are only two children, and the boy is quite
a little fellow yet.'

'That is just the difficulty. Will it not look as if I
were marrying the girl for her money ?'

'Nobody will say that of my son,' answered Mr.
Lascelles proudly. 'The Lascelles are a much older
family than the Woodalls. He is the best fellow in
the world, and one of my oldest friends ; but between
you and me, Ronald, I don't believe he has a grandfather.'

'Not now, I dare say,' said Ronald, smiling. 'Why,
he is at least fifty. But no doubt he had a grandfather
some time or other.'

'Quite a nonentity, then—a man no one ever heard of. Probably a grocer in the City. Now you, Ronald, have ancestors to be proud of. Admiral Sir Ronald Lascelles burnt the French fleet at——'

'Oh yes, father, I know all about Admiral Sir Ronald, and General Lascelles who was Governor of Virginia under George I., and all that. But people really do not attach much weight to an historical name nowadays, unless there is a handle to it, or money as well.'

'I am afraid not, Ronald,' assented the Consul.

'Then, as a matter of fact, and looking at it calmly and impartially, what have I to offer in exchange for Miss Woodall's money and the position her father might make for me? It is no use pretending. I don't want to deceive myself: I have nothing at all to offer—neither a title, nor position, nor money, nor talents.'

'Plenty of talent, my boy,' said Mr. Lascelles. 'Do not make yourself out too cheap.'

'No, father; that is not my way. I am generally bumptious enough. But somehow I have not fancied myself quite so much lately as I used to.'

'So it seems,' observed the Consul, with a little touch of sarcasm.

'And,' continued the young man, 'though I believe I have a certain amount of brains, they have wasted dreadfully in that wretched office. If I had hammered away at writing for the papers, or plays, or poetry, like some of the fellows did, I might have acquired some sort of reputation. But I wasted the time sadly.'

'Do you really mean that because the girl you love has money, and you have none at present, you will give her up ?' asked Mr. Lascelles.

'I think I ought, as a gentleman,' said Ronald. 'Besides, I have told you that I am not so sure about loving her.'

‘That is all fudge!’ exclaimed his father almost impatiently. ‘If anyone is to be judged by his conduct, you are very much in love with her indeed. The other question is far more serious. You are quite right to consult me about it, because it is one of those questions in which women cannot as a rule give a reliable opinion, however clever they may be. But I am pretty well certain that you need have no scruples.’

‘Why, father?’

‘Because the girl is, I believe, much attached to you. You have not intrigued nor sneaked to gain her affection——’

‘No, indeed!’ exclaimed Ronald.

‘Exactly. Circumstances have brought it about that you have become a sort of hero in the place, which, by-the-by, is more than you deserve for having been such a young donkey,’ said Mr. Lascelles good-humouredly. ‘That Italian might just as well have killed you altogether. But nobody supposes, nobody can suppose, that the duel was part of a premeditated plan.'

'Of course not,' assented the young man.

'Well, your mother tells me that Miss Woodall is thoroughly in love with you, and will accept you at once if you propose.'

'I am not so sure of that,' remarked Ronald.

'If she refuses you, there is an end of the matter,' Mr. Lascelles went on. 'Then, of course, we must take measures to find you something to do, and the sooner you get away from here the better. But I think your mother is right; she generally is.'

'Yes, father.'

'And I believe that Woodall would not mind a bit. On the contrary, I think he would sooner give his daughter to you than to anyone else.'

'You are very sanguine, father dear, and you think too well of me.'

'No, my boy; but I know Woodall. He does not like the Italians, and as Edith has kept house for him here since his wife's death, she has, of course, not seen much of English society. She has not made the acquaintance of any very eligible young men. So you have a very fair field and practically no competitors at present.'

'That is all quite true,' assented Ronald.

'Then, if the father likes you, and sees no objection in your having neither money nor position, and if the daughter likes you, and will be wretched if you don't propose——'

'Oh! she is not so far gone as that,' interrupted the young man.

'Your mother thinks so,' retorted the Consul; 'and she is generally right. Of course, however, she *may* be mistaken. In that case, as I said before, no harm is done, and you will go away, as you would probably do under other circumstances, as soon as you are well.'

'Certainly,' answered Ronald. 'It is no use stopping here doing nothing.'

'Precisely. Now let me finish what I was going to say. If father and daughter both like you, he moderately and she very much indeed, and if they don't mind your being penniless, why the deuce should you worry about it, eh ?'

'It does seem rather absurd,' said Ronald.

'It *is* absurd. Make up your mind, my boy. You won't do better, I can tell you. We should all be pleased; and think how happy your mother would be. But now I must really get down to the Consulate.'

This was the last mesh in the net. Mr. Lascelles had taken much more time and trouble to discuss the matter than his son had expected, and he had argued it out fairly and sensibly, without any special paternal bias. Ronald could not see any flaw in the reasoning. There was certainly a vast difference between an ordinary fortune-hunter and a young man of good name but small means, who happened to please a wealthy young lady and her father. No one could possibly accuse him of having tried to win Edith for her money's sake. As Stornello and Donati had told him, the feeling was all the other way, and people thought that Edith was lucky to get such a hero for a husband.

Ronald knew very well in his heart that he was not a hero, and before the visits he had received he had had no notion of being considered one. But when a man is exposed to continuous subtle flattery for several days consecutively, he is rather apt to forget his own intimate convictions, and to estimate himself at the high value set on him by his friends. It was not an unpleasant feeling, and though the idol might know that he was but clay, it was decidedly nice to be placed on a pedestal and worshipped, and assured that he was all pure gold.

That he was in love with Edith he now supposed must be true, for everybody said he was; that she was in love with him he concluded to be probable, as he trusted his mother's judgment implicitly on this subject; that Mr. Woodall would accept him as a son-in-law also appeared likely, from what his father and Stornello had told him. And as all Portino thought him a hero, perhaps after all he was heroic without knowing it. St. Clair, and Egerton Paull, and a dozen other men, would have done just the same, he thought. Perhaps they were all heroes, only that they had not been so lucky as himself in having opportunities of proving it.

CHAPTER XVI.

A CHARADE.

WHEN Mrs. Lascelles found her son in a pliable state of mind, she lost no time in making use of it. Towards the middle of May many families annually left Portino for the hills. It was now already April, so there were not many weeks to waste. Ronald was progressing very well, but it would be some time before he could walk. He could not yet be lifted into a carriage and driven to the Palazzo Woodall to make his proposal. Nor, on the other hand, could she invite Edith to come to his sofa and be proposed to.

Her ingenuity was, however, quite equal to the

emergency. She sallied forth one fine day very soon after the conversation between father and son (which, of course, had been reported to her in *précis* form) to see her dear friend Edith, whose numerous visits of inquiry she had not yet rewarded by a single call. The girl was at home, and Mrs. Lascelles was at once shown into her sitting-room, where she was practising industriously on the piano. At the sight of her visitor Edith started up, and, turning pale, exclaimed :

'He is not worse, is he ?'

Mrs. Lascelles smiled, and kissed her affectionately.

'No, dear ; thank God, he is really quite well, only he is not allowed to use his leg at all, and, of course, he cannot leave the sofa at present.'

'Oh, I am so glad !' said Edith, her colour returning. 'Do sit down, Mrs. Lascelles. How good of you to come and see me !'

'I have come to consult you, dear.'

' Yes ?   About what ?'

' About Ronald.'   Edith blushed again.   ' You see, he is dreadfully dull.   So would any young man be, confined to a couch all day, and not able even to fetch a book for himself.'

' Of course,' assented Edith ; ' it must be dreadful for him.'

' Yes,' continued Mrs. Lascelles.   'Some of his friends come to see him occasionally, and Teresina and I do our best to amuse him ; but he is dull all the same, and the doctors say that his spirits ought to be kept up.   He is so used to activity, you know !   When he is in good health he is always playing cricket, or sailing, or rowing, and it is very hard for him to be mewed up in two rooms.'

' Very hard indeed,' said the girl ; ' I wonder he bears it patiently.'

' Oh, he is wonderfully good and patient !' exclaimed Mrs. Lascelles, intent on praising up her man.

'Men are generally so tiresome when they are ill, always fidgeting and grumbling. Now Ronald is as gentle and good-tempered as an angel. But he is very dull, all the same. He wants a little amusement.'

'What do you propose to do, Mrs. Lascelles? How can I help you? I wish I could. I would do anything in my power for you.'

Edith was careful to offer her help to the mother, for the mother's sake. A month ago she would have said frankly that she would do anything in her power to help Ronald. But love teaches girls caution.

'I am sure you would, dear,' said Mrs. Lascelles, again kissing her. 'That is why I have come to you. Now this is what I propose : You know we have a boudoir behind the drawing-room—the little room looking on the courtyard?'

'Yes,' said Miss Woodall; 'well?'

'Well, we hardly ever use the room, though it is

separated from the drawing-room only by folding doors. Mr. Lascelles had them nailed up and covered with a curtain, because he thought they made the place draughty. But of course, now the fine weather has come, they could be opened again easily.'

'I know the place,' said Edith; 'we used to act charades there when we were children.'

'Exactly, replied Mrs. Lascelles. 'Now, Ronald wants a little amusement, you know, and I thought it would be such a capital idea if we got up a little charade again. Just a trifle to cheer him up, you know, and divert his thoughts, for the poor fellow has lost his berth in Somerset House.'

'Lost it!' exclaimed Edith. 'How?'

'On account of his illness, dear. He was obliged to ask for two months' more leave, and they would not give it him.'

'Why not? How cruel!'

'It *was* unkind. Some wretched gossip told his

chief the reason of Ronald's illness, and it seems they disapprove of duels very strongly.'

'Then he was punished for his bravery?' said Edith. 'Oh dear, how dreadful!'

'That is over now, my dear, and it is no use lamenting,' said Mrs. Lascelles, who saw by Edith's disturbed face that her shot had hit the mark. 'What we must do is to try and amuse the dear boy, and get him to forget his trouble. Unless he does, he will be a long time getting better. At least that is what Salviati thinks.'

Dr. Salviati may have thought it, but he certainly had not said so. The patient was prohibited from moving his leg at all, and had to adhere to an invalid diet. Beyond this, and a general order not to excite himself, the doctor's instructions did not go. There was now no longer the slightest fear of fever.

'I shall be very glad to do what I can,' said Edith, 'but people will be going away soon.'

'Oh! I am thinking only of quite a simple little charade, something that you and Teresina, and your brother Charley, and perhaps young Donati, might get up between you. We should only just ask a few intimate friends. Charley will be back soon, will he not?'

'We expect him to-morrow, Good Friday,' answered Edith. 'His holidays will last about three weeks, but he will have to go away again on Tuesday fortnight.'

'That suits exactly,' Mrs. Lascelles went on. 'We should not want more than a week's preparation for this sort of thing. The rehearsals and so on would amuse Ronald. We could put him on his sofa in the boudoir, with his little table by his side, and he would enjoy the fun immensely, I know.'

'I am afraid I could not act,' said Edith hesitatingly; 'I should be too nervous. I have not done such a thing for years.'

'Nonsense, dear! we could not get on without you at all. You really must! you know, you promised to do what you could to help us.'

'But I did not expect this; and I don't know whether papa could spare me.'

Edith was, in truth, doubtful about the whole affair. A flush of joy had come over her when the plan was suggested; as it would enable her to see Ronald, and to convince herself that he was really getting well, and to tell him how she repented her flirtation with Della Rocca, which had caused all his misfortune. But then doubts had assailed her. Would she be able to act at all? Would it be proper to discuss the duel with Ronald? Would her father allow her to go? Her cogitations were interrupted by Mrs. Lascelles.

'You must choose the piece, my dear, and arrange it, and select the actors, and everything. And as to your father, I will go at once and ask his leave. So

that is settled.   Now, good-bye! Come round on
Saturday with Charley and we will have a talk
over it.'

Mr. Woodall was rather surprised when Mrs. Lascelles's card was brought into his private room.   For
a moment he thought that the lady came as an ambassador to negotiate an alliance for her son. He had
a great respect for her talents, and felt that he would
be at a decided disadvantage.   When she came in and
said at once: 'You are astonished to see me at
the Bank, Mr. Woodall!   I have come to ask
a great favour,' he was more alarmed than ever.
He said:

'Sit down, Mrs. Lascelles! Very happy to oblige
you in any way I can.   I hope your son is getting on
nicely!' But he did not feel happy, and did not
look it.

'He is very dull,' replied Mrs. Lascelles. 'Teresina
is going to try a little charade to amuse her brother—

quite a children's thing, you know. I want you to let Edith and Charley help her.'

Mr. Woodall breathed again. Not because he had felt any hostility to the proposal he had expected, but because he did not like the idea of discussing it with so superior a woman as Mrs. Lascelles, and thought she would certainly obtain from him promises and concessions for which he might be sorry afterwards. The banker was so pleased at being let off this time that he raised no objection whatever, and willingly gave his children leave to attend rehearsals as often as Mrs. Lascelles liked. The latter sent a triumphant note to Edith, who meanwhile had been dwelling in agony of mind on the information imparted to her. Her self-reproaches had been bitter enough before, for she had blamed her flippancy and flirtation with Della Rocca as the cause of Ronald's serious wound; but now they were much worse. For she had also been the cause of his losing his position in Somerset House.

She did not exactly know what the appointment was worth, but the 'Civil Service' sounds well, and she thought it might have led to something grand and worthy of Ronald.

Now his years of hard, tedious work and his prospects were all gone, and lost through her fault! How could Mrs. Lascelles be so good to her? If she only knew all, she would not even speak to the wicked cause of her son's misfortunes. And they were quite beyond her power to remedy. She, poor girl, could do nothing to make Ronald amends. She could not compensate him for the years wasted and the hopes dashed to the ground. Then a sudden thought flashed across her mind. Money! of course she had money. Her mother had left her ten thousand pounds! Could she contrive to give it to him without being found out? A miserable four hundred a year would of course not half make up for Ronald's suffering and disappointments, but it would help to make his life bearable, and to prevent his cursing her too deeply. But how should she manage? Her father and Mr. Lascelles were the trustees, and she believed that she could not deal with the capital without their consent, which of course they would not give. But she might send him the interest every half-year anonymously, and let him know that he might always reckon on it. For poor Edith now no longer dared to think of the possibility which, a few weeks before, had made her tell her first falsehood. Of course, Ronald must hate her; he could not do otherwise. He would detest the very sight of her, and it would, she thought, be a sore trial to him that she should come to the Consulate to help in the charade. But she was determined to drink her bitter cup to its very dregs.

She would tell him how deeply she repented the thoughtlessness which had had such grave consequences, and she would beg his forgiveness. He might be hard, and might not pardon her at once, but at some future time, when he had got a good appointment, he would think better of her for having told him frankly and humbly of her great sorrow.

When Charley Woodall arrived at Portino he was delighted with the prospect of fun held out to him. All Saturday he and his sister, with Teresina, were rummaging among old books, trying to find an appropriate charade, or some little comedy which might be cut down to the required dimensions. By the evening they had discovered about a dozen that might do, if altered and pruned, but not one which was absolutely and certainly the right one.

Teresina proposed to take them home and let Ronald look at them. 'You and Charley come in after dinner,' she said, 'and then we will all consult with mamma and Ronald. He is very clever about such things.'

Edith only half consented. She might be willing

to come and rehearse, but she would not make herself quite at home at the Consulate by walking in at all hours. She pleaded that Mrs. Lascelles might not like it, that probably Ronald should not be disturbed, and so on. But as soon as Teresina showed her bundle of little books to her mother, and reported Edith's hesitation, old Luisa was sent off with a pressing note which admitted of no refusal.

At eight o'clock Charley and Edith appeared in the drawing-room at the Consulate. Both Mr. and Mrs. Lascelles were present, and the latter had been careful not to make the young girl uncomfortable. Ronald was still upstairs, on a sofa in his father's study, which had been appropriated entirely to his own use. Young Donati was with him. So, after a short chat, which turned entirely on the merits of the pieces suggested, Mrs. Lascelles took the young people upstairs.

Before so many eyes Edith could do nothing but

shake hands with Ronald, and hope he was better. It went like a knife through her heart to feel how thin and weak was that hand, which had pressed her own with such warmth and strength when he handed her into the carriage after the Donati's ball. The room was not too brilliantly lighted—Ronald's sofa was in the shadow. So she hoped that no one noticed the deep blush she felt, in her endeavour to make her greeting an ordinary one.

'Thank you so much for the roses; they have been very sweet to me.' This was all that Ronald said.

'How good of him!' she thought. 'He conceals his aversion, and is quite civil, because all the family are here.'

Then the plays were discussed, and Ronald listened to the discussions and threw in a word now and then. By-and-by he became quite interested, and showed them how one piece would not do, because it required too many changes of scene, and another would be unsuitable because they had not enough men. Finally, he proposed adapting a short French *proverbe.*

'But who will translate it?' asked Teresina. 'I don't know French enough, and I'm not sufficiently clever.'

'If you will do the actual writing, Teresina, I will dictate,' said Ronald. 'I can do it capitally from the sofa.'

The idea was received with acclamation, and it was decided that the work should begin on Monday morning. But the distribution of parts required some thought. In the *proverbe* there was a hero and his mother, a heroine and her father, and a comic valet. After much discussion, in which Edith scarcely joined, it was decided that Donati should play the hero, Edith the heroine, Teresina the hero's mother' and Stornello the heroine's father, while little Charley should take the valet. Probably the cast would have been different if Edith had not objected strongly to play heroine to Stornello as *premier amoureux*. She would not be suspected of flirting again, even in fun, and with Stornello there might possibly be some notion of the sort. Donati was too young for any such suspicion. Teresina herself volunteered to act the old lady, which she was much more likely to do well than the enamoured heroine. Girls of sixteen cannot, as a rule, act young parts as well as very old ones. The interval between sixteen and nineteen is very small in some respects, enormous in others.

The party separated in good spirits late at night Only Edith had been quiet and subdued.

END OF VOL. I.

BILLING AND SONS, PRINTERS, GUILDFORD.